RACING FROM DANGER

LEANNE MALLOY

RACING FROM DANGER

PALMETTO
P U B L I S H I N G
Charleston, SC
www.PalmettoPublishing.com

Racing from Danger
Copyright © 2024 by Leanne Malloy

First Edition

Paperback ISBN: 979-8-8229-3738-3
eBook ISBN: 979-8-8229-3739-0

Content Advisory: Some scenes in this book depict violence against a
female. Be assured that she is strong and resilient!

This book is a work of fiction. Names, characters, businesses,
places, events, and incidents are either the products of the author's
imagination or used in a fictitious manner. Any resemblance to actual
persons or actual events is purely coincidental.

This book is dedicated to all helpers, whether they be medical, psychological, spiritual, law enforcement, or first responders. Their work saves countless lives, often in ways unknown.

CHAPTER ONE

KIMBERLY NEWTON PUNCHED IN the security code and entered her friend's high-end condominium on the northside of Indianapolis. As always, she relished her new side hustle: walking dogs while their owners toiled at their jobs in downtown Indy. Clad in an old T-shirt and yoga pants, she enjoyed the physical and emotional freedom the clothes provided. Better yet, since her principal role as a psychologist was performed in the comfort of her home via telehealth, she needed only to top her pants with a casual sweater and jacket to be ready for work this evening.

It was a glorious spring day. May in Indiana meant green grass, colorful flowers, and of course allergies for those who suffered from them. Walking Russ Kellams's goofy Goldendoodle, Reed, in such beautiful weather was hardly something she should charge for. Russ should be paying *her* for the pleasure of getting low impact exercise and interacting with his sweet dog. Such blessings almost made her forget the events of the past several months.

Thanking God for the relative safety of her job, she shuddered at the memories that crowded her brain. *At least I came out of it mostly unharmed. My credit rating is clear and the man who hurt me is behind bars.*

Unfortunately, once her brain had begun to focus on Tom Adams it wouldn't stop until she processed it all, yet again. The day in question had been busy with back-to-back patients, so busy that she'd allowed herself to get dehydrated by bedtime. Dog-walking, pet-sitting, and a full roster of late afternoon and evening clients had made her more than parched. She went to bed with a baby migraine, hoping to feel better in the morning. No such luck. At 2am her phone had jingled. The emergency department at a downtown hospital was calling for her consultation services.

At the ED she had assessed Adams to determine the need for hospitalization. Throughout their hour-long session, he had alternately feigned being strung out, suicidal, and homeless. Because Adams was remarkably good-looking, some of the ED nurses were sympathetic to his cause. The doctors, on the other hand, doubted Adams's story.

When Kim refused Adams admission to the hospital, arranging a referral to a nearby drug rehab facility that would send a caseworker to transport him to their building, Adams begged and flattered. When those appeals to her clinical expertise and vanity failed, his demeanor changed. He became less vulnerable and more dogmatic about his need for "just a few nights in a hospital bed." He wasn't in need of drug abuse treatment, he pleaded, only a period of quiet and rest. He began to outline his extensive family history, which to Kim's ears sounded sad but not extreme. Her gut told her Adams wasn't coddled enough by his parents, therefore in his mind he was abused.

At that point, another patient came into the ED suffering with gunshot wounds. The entire staff rushed to another room to tend to him. Adams became frustrated at their "abandonment," which Kim gently confronted. She noted the patient had life threatening wounds, and that Adams's needs were being met. His eyes briefly deadened before he was able to become charming again, concerned for the victim in the next room. Kim was struck by his lack of empathy.

Her training kicked in as she remembered the characteristics of psychopaths. Family, religion, spirituality, and concern for others were only of use if they could meet the person's needs. Goals and future plans were primary, as opposed to past events. Finally, psychopaths tended to mimic the expressions of others, which was precisely what Adams had done when he saw Kim's concern for the gunshot victim.

While the drum solo continued to throb in her head, she reviewed the options for Tom Adams. He could be released or transported to the treatment center. His blood work had come back from the lab, and all results were normal per the nurse who delivered them. That opened up the third option of the homeless shelter a few blocks away, which Adams angrily refused.

Adams didn't strike out, nor did he threaten her or the staff. He just stared at Kim as if trying to remember everything about her face. As he left the ED he said, "I'll be seeing you, Dr. Newton. It was good to get to know you. We'll meet again." And for the first time that night, she was afraid.

During their many sessions together after Adams's imprisonment, her pastor had both comforted her and reminded her that this was a fallen world, that God let humans have free will, and therefore bad things would happen. He reminded Kim that God was still with her in all trials. The basic, almost simplistic theology had been all Kim could absorb at the time. It had taken several months, but she was almost at the place where she could believe God was good in all things. Almost.

Willing herself to focus on the present, she eyed the interior of Russ's condominium. The furniture in this home delighted her. While most of her clients, including Russ, were affluent, this residence was different. Comfort was key, with many of the design elements second-hand or passed on by family members. The furnishings in her place could also boast of similar humble origins due to her greedy ex-husband, but the style here was second to none. Color tied everything together, even the two crazy unmatched recliners, one in an abstract floral fabric and the other in a Scottish plaid. If she'd tried this, the effect would have been awful. But Russ, her client, self-trained decorator, and the condo owner, had the knack. Reds and greens hooked the styles together without causing Christmas carols to pop into her head. How did he do that?

As she wove her way into the kitchen, a faint sweet smell greeted her. Sweet, but also sickly, if that was a descriptor. And where was Reed, the doodle she was supposed to take on his daily walk? He usually bounded into her the minute the lock tripped on the front door. Then she heard a sad whimper, which she knew to be Reed's.

"Where are you, my good boy?" she asked. "Kim's here to take you out. We're going to have a grand time today. It's sunny and clear, the best Indiana spring day ever."

Whimpering answered her for a second time, followed by a low growl. She began to worry. Reed wasn't coming to greet her. Something was wrong; maybe he was ill. Doodles had delicate stomachs sometimes. She'd cleaned her share of doggy poop and puddles on her job, which was part of the drill. But the odor she was smelling, while foul, wasn't poop. And Reed rarely growled.

As she turned the corner to the screened porch overlooking the condo development's large lake, Reed greeted her with a faint wag of his tail. He remained seated on his haunches, next to a mound of something partially covered in the shadows. Kim recognized the tarp as Russ's grill cover. Kim was concerned that Russ would leave the porch so messy. Maybe he was ill, not the dog.

She began to soothe Reed when she felt a sharp pain in the back of her head. Hitting the floor, she heard a man's voice say something. The voice was guttural, angry, and gleeful all at once, the words garbled. Then Kim heard nothing.

— — — — — — — — — — — — —

"Miss, can you hear me?" a different male voice asked. "Can you open your eyes?" Daniel Westbrook, a detective with the Indianapolis Metropolitan Police Department, looked at the pretty woman with the bloody gashes at the base of her head and front hairline. Her hair was matted with blood and she was stirring. The EMT was hovering, wanting to get her to the hospital, but Dan wasn't about to let the opportunity for a witness's fresh account slip by. The other victim, evidently the owner of the condo, was being wheeled out on a gurney, still unconscious. According to the lead paramedic, he would be fine. The stab wound in his side missed important organs but had caused significant blood loss. Dan's best guess was that the attractive woman had walked in on the crime scene while the perp was still present, rendering him or her unable to finish the job.

A search of her car and purse had yielded her name: Kimberly Newton. She also had an Indiana psychologist card in her wallet. *Great, a psych type. He'd never get a straight answer from her. Just his luck.*

Almost every psychologist or therapist he'd encountered began their answer to a question with, "Well, it depends." The marriage and family therapist he and his ex-wife had gone to was also a pro at hedging. And he was a guy, to boot! Dan had expected a little more support from another male.

But no, the problems in the marriage were all about Dan's long work hours, his preoccupation with his job, and his "lack of emotional availability." What was that supposed to mean? Well, basically it meant he was now divorced.

Time had helped. Dan and his ex were cordial, their tenuous relationship helped by the fact they'd had no children. He'd lost his portion of their house but was otherwise unscathed financially. Deb, his former wife, had recently married a guy who worked remotely. Her need for constant attention was perfectly satisfied by a husband able to throw in a load of laundry, cook, and focus on her during his work breaks.

Dan knew he was being unfair. Deb was a good person, just profoundly needy. Her new husband's job allowed them to eat three meals each day together. Dan laughed. On his job he was lucky to get one meal on the run. That meal was usually full of grease and came in a paper bag.

He had to focus. Dr. Newton was trying to wake up, and he needed a statement from her. The first responder was taking her vitals and didn't seem concerned, which he hoped would allow for some serious questioning. He had many questions.

"What happened?" the woman asked. "Who are you?"

"I'm Daniel Westbrook, from IMPD," he answered slowly. "You've been attacked. If you're up to it, I need to hear what happened."

The EMT, Randy, eased her up into a sitting position, which resulted in her vomiting into the bag he had ready. "She's got a concussion, for sure, Dan," Randy said. "We've got to get her to the ED for a scan and a better work-up than I can provide here. You can talk to her after that."

"I'll talk to her while you take her to the ambulance," Dan said. His tone allowed for no argument.

"I can tell you what I know," Kim said, as she reclined on the gurney and wiped her mouth with the tissue Randy provided. "I was here to walk Russ's dog. Reed was whimpering next to what I assume was Russ's body. Then I got hit." She paused for a beat, and added, "Is Russ okay? Was he under the grill cover? What about Reed? Did he get hurt?"

Randy chimed in, as much to soothe Kim as to answer. "Russ will be fine. The dog is with a neighbor. It's best if you stay quiet. You've got two skin wounds and quite a goose egg forming."

"Yeah, I've got a fierce headache. Probably a concussion, huh? And tossing my cookies in front of all my new friends is so embarrassing."

Even Dan laughed. In addition to being a great-looking woman, she had grit. He'd reserve judgment on how helpful she would be to his investigation. Her clothing indicated a lack of the usual focus on professional wear, so maybe she was halfway normal. But if she tried to psychoanalyze her attacker while making excuses for vague childhood angst, he'd reign her in. The crew wheeled her out and he got in his car to follow the ambulance to the hospital. As he'd expected, he was barred from the emergency department.

– – – – – – – – – – – – – – –

Several hours later Dan returned to the hospital, after attempting to chip away at the mountain of paperwork on his desk. After consulting with the woman at the kiosk in the lobby for Kim's whereabouts, he finally found her room. A glance into the open doorway revealed her sitting up in bed sipping some broth. The nurse in charge intercepted him before he could enter. Evidently, Kim had been admitted from the ED to the med-surg floor for observation.

"She's exhausted and her head is throbbing, but she's putting on a good front," the silver-haired nurse said. "Go easy on her. She keeps trying to figure out what she could have done to help her friend. As if. Some folks are just no darn good."

Dan nodded and wondered where older nurses got the idea they could boss everybody around. Probably from being able to do it, and because they were usually the most knowledgeable people in the room. "Thanks for your input," he said. Knowing she'd been disrespected, she arched her brow and turned to go to the patient room next door.

Easing himself into the hard chair at the bedside, Dan studied Dr. Kim Newton. Still very nice looking, despite the bruising beginning to form over her lower face and the stitches the plastic surgeon had been careful to apply to the gash at the front of her face near the hairline. He'd noted that injury when he'd talked to her at the crime scene. Blue eyes contrasted nicely with her dark hair. He noted a few strands of gray in the long waves and estimated her age at close to his, mid to late thirties. The vintage Beatles T-shirt and tight, stretchy pants were gone, replaced by a hospital gown, which he thought was a shame. As he was making his observations, Kim's eyes squinted.

"Assessing me?" she asked. "How do I stack up? Trustworthy? Ditzy female? Stupid for entering a place where a criminal was hard at work?"

Dan pasted a bland smile on his face. "How about a little paranoid? Dr. Newton, I'm Dan Westbrook. I doubt you remember me from the condo. I need to follow up with more questions."

Kim blinked and smiled. "Good assessment, Detective Westbrook. Paranoid is the perfect word to describe me right now. But I'll bounce back. Yes, I remember you and promise not to vomit this time around. Ask your questions."

Dan smiled, more genuinely this time. "Let's begin with what happened. Why were you in Mr. Kellams's home?"

"I'm his dog walker," Kim replied. "He was supposed to be on a flight to North Carolina for a furniture outlet sale."

Dan studied her. Crease lines formed on her forehead while she tried to remember the details of Russ's whereabouts. As he hoped, she continued.

"Russ is an interior decorator. There's a big furniture show in Jamestown. He goes a few times a year and snags bargain pieces for his business. He's very talented, as you could probably see from his home."

"His decor wasn't my priority," Dan said. "So, you were there to walk his dog, but Russ was there, too. Why?"

"I have no clue. Maybe he forgot something. He's notorious for getting to the airport hours before he has to, so he would have had time to rush home to retrieve something."

"That's actually correct. Mr. Kellams told us he forgot his phone. Please continue."

Kim rolled her eyes, as if annoyed she'd had to pass some sort of test with him. "I was surprised that Reed, Russ's dog, didn't greet me at the door. He was whimpering in the sunroom. I saw a tarp covering something, then I heard someone speaking, and then I was talking to you. That's all I've got. Sorry."

"What did you hear?"

"Words. I couldn't make them out." She took the ice pack and placed it carefully on her forehead, breathing deeply. "Whatever he said, it sounded mean. Menacing. Cruel."

"You're sure it was a male voice?"

"Yes, I'm sure."

Dan watched Kim breathe. She was exhaling through slightly pursed lips, which meant she was in pain. Nurse Bossy would probably be in soon with meds for Kim and a scolding for him. He needed to keep pushing. "What do you know about Mr. Kellams? Any enemies?"

"Russ is an angel," she said softly. "He's kind, trustworthy, and even friends with his ex-wife. They co-parent their son with a lot of grace. I can't imagine him having an enemy with violent tendencies."

Now she was talking like a shrink. Terrific. "Well, you can't know what motivated his attacker, can you? What about enemies with *nonviolent* tendencies?"

Glaring at him, Kim answered after a pause. "Russ is a talented decorator, as I said. Some in the Indianapolis interior design community resent his success. He's entirely self-taught. He doesn't have training or certification, which galls a lot of people. But again, I doubt they'd attack him."

"Come on, Dr. Newton. Work with me. Surely there's someone resentful enough of Mr. Kellams to have done this. Maybe he's gotten an award they thought they deserved? Or perhaps his ex has a new lover who dislikes him? Or he dislikes that the new lover will be providing primary care for his son? There are infinite possibilities. We *all* have enemies."

"Well, I'm sure *you* do," Kim said, pressing her call button. "I doubt Russ does."

Nurse Bossy entered so quickly Dan was sure she'd been outside the door. "Enough," she said. "Dr. Newton is tired and in pain. I said to go easy, but you didn't care to listen. You can leave now, or I'll call security. *And* I'll have your supervisor paged at IMPD."

Dan stood and shrugged. Noting the grin on Kim's battered face, he added, "I'll be checking back with you, Dr. Newton. They say you'll be released tomorrow morning. I expect you to cooperate when you're asked to give a written statement at headquarters."

Kim saluted, he laughed, and he was ushered out by the nurse. Feeling mildly guilty because he'd known Kim was in pain and continued to question her, he decided to have a late supper in the hospital. He was no cook and the aroma as he passed the cafeteria was surprisingly good. It beat eating alone at his place.

Dr. Newton's salute caused him to conjecture Deb's possible response to a heavy-handed order from him. There was no way in the world Deb would have saluted after he'd issued a command when she was in a hospital bed. She would have been alternately tearful, angry, and pouty. Kim Newton was certainly not Deb.

No, Kim Newton was a tough woman, tough enough that she could find humor in the bizarre situation she'd landed in. Not so tough she'd neglected to ask about Russ Kellams, and even his dog. What kind of human was that thoughtful when she had a concussion and was bleeding from two different wounds? Dr. Newton was a puzzle.

A very attractive puzzle to be sure. Her face was beautiful, even with the bloody smears and the skin discoloration that would get worse before it got better. And under the baggy gown was a fine figure. She was also very intelligent, based on her responses to his questions. And she was playful but unwilling to take much from him, as she noted he probably had plenty of enemies, unlike her friend Russ. In any other setting, Dan would like very much to get to know Dr. Newton better.

This was not that setting. He had work to do. In all likelihood, Dr. Newton would return to her psych sensibilities as the investigation continued. She'd analyze the criminal he was searching for, providing no helpful input as she drilled down on the creep's probable tragic upbringing. It was time to center in on the investigation. After he'd eaten, of course.

Dan walked to the cafeteria and thought again about Kim's statement that he probably had enemies. He and Deb weren't enemies. Lots of people he'd sent to prison certainly were. But he slept well at night, his conscience clear of guilt or second-guessing.

Except about his parents. The guilt remained. He'd done everything but spirit their car away in the middle of the night. His dad had finally convinced him he'd call a ride share for any night driving needs. Dad had lied. Now he and Dan's mother were dead. The combination of darkness, rain, and his father's anxiety about his wife's chest pains had resulted in a head-on crash into a utility pole.

He'd been assured they hadn't suffered. His agony persisted anyway. Even his younger sister believed she and Dan had done what they could to keep their parents safe. But they hadn't.

Despite the tasty quesadilla and guac, he chewed without enjoyment. He continued to ruminate as he returned his tray with its numerous empty plates to the collection belt. Nurse Bossy appeared from behind him and took his arm. "Detective Westbrook let's sit a minute. I'll bring my food over in a second."

Dan obliged. Watching Nurse Bossy navigate the food court's tasty offerings, he wondered about her. What had led her to hospital nursing? How did she maintain her motivation after what appeared to be a long career? He often did this, asking himself questions about others' history and life circumstances. Most important, what did she want with him?

"I'm Betty Shields," she said by way of introduction as she sat opposite him at a small corner table. "I wanted to apologize, a little, for my protective behavior with Kim. She's a wonderful woman and was a real asset to our hospital. Kim did after hours emergency room assessments for five years, until she opened her telehealth practice. We really miss her."

"Why did she quit? Better money treating private clients?" Even Dan knew he was being too cynical, but he felt compelled to ask. Kim Newton didn't strike him as a quitter.

Betty eyed him with a hint of distaste. "No, she had a bad experience with one of the patients she assessed. He was an emergency room floater, seeking drugs, a bed in our psych unit, the chance to seduce vulnerable women on staff, and a few days of free meals. More than that, he was a big faker, one who liked to test young staffers with his stories. Kim had him pegged and he resented it."

She chewed on her salad and had a bite of garlic bread. "You see, he didn't look like the 'usual' drug seeker." After using air quotes while she talked, Betty crunched a few more bites of her chicken and pecan salad and continued. "Tom Adams could have been a *GQ* model. Sandy blonde hair, great physique, perfect teeth. He was dressed for the golf course, complete with a popped collar on his polo shirt and madras shorts. It was all a carefully constructed facade. Mind you, Kim's got a kind heart and is very understanding of folks with depression and addiction issues. But this guy was obviously trying to game the system and had a lawyer on speed dial. The ED staff needed Kim's corroboration before they discharged him. Boy, did she pay for doing the right thing."

"What happened?" Dan's stomach tightened.

"Nothing at first," Betty said after a long pause. "But a few months later, she discovered her identity had been stolen. At about the same time, Adams sued her for negligent care. You can guess the rest. She spent the better part of a year clearing her credit. Legal fees were horrendous. Her malpractice insurance company eventually settled, saying it was easier than a trial to prove her lack of negligence, but she really suffered. A *lot*. And she quit the ED job. Can't say I blame her a bit."

Betty continued to eat her supper, topping off the salad with a piece of coconut cream pie. Dan thought about calling Betty out for her incongruous food choices but decided against it. She would not appreciate his judgment.

"After her divorce from the useless womanizer she married in grad school, Kim thought she had her life on track again. No such luck. And now this attack." Betty took her first bite of pie and said, "Here's the thing, Detective. Kim deserves more respect than you're giving her. My guess is you've had a bad experience with a therapist and you're taking it out on her."

Dan's face reddened. After a beat he admitted, "You're correct, Betty. I'll make it right with Dr. Newton. Thanks for your input." He grinned. "This time I mean it."

They parted as friends, or at least what passed for friendship with Nurse Betty. On his drive home, Dan considered what he'd learned of Kim's past. She was an experienced psychologist but had been scared away from hospital work by a probable psychopath. Given what he knew about that type, he guessed other things had happened to Kim that Betty might not know. He hoped she hadn't been sexually assaulted or otherwise injured. Whatever had occurred, she was a strong woman. Slamming his hand on the steering wheel, he berated himself. He hadn't asked Betty if Dr. Newton's ex-husband was physically abusive during their marriage. Nor had he asked if the ED patient had been sentenced and jailed. Hopefully he had. And he wondered who else on Kim's client list could want to harm her.

CHAPTER TWO

KIM'S FRIEND AND NEIGHBOR, Adele Foley, arrived at her hospital room the next morning with a change of clothing and Kim's makeup bag. After a quick hug, Kim went to the bathroom to shower, change, and tend to her battered appearance.

When she was cleaned up, she made a slow twirl and teased the eighty-something-year-old woman. "What do you think of my work with heavy-duty concealer, Adele? Will I scare my patients when I see them on screen? Or should I postpone their sessions until next week?"

"Not funny, missy," Adele answered, using the nickname she favored for Kim. "I happen to know you've already rescheduled them all via your phone app. For a few weeks out. You told me when I called last night, but your concussion is affecting your memory. My job now is to get you through this. Your nurse gave me quite a list of instructions, which include my staying over at your place for the next few nights."

Kim teared up. "That's a lot to ask of you, Adele. Are you sure you're up to it? I can stay at your place if that's better for you. We can order takeout. If we stay at my house, you don't have to do any housework or cooking. All I really need from you is your care and company."

"*Takeout?*" Adele asked, as if Kim had uttered an obscenity. "I think not. I've already got two casseroles in your freezer. Tonight's menu will be grilled cheese and tomato soup because you need bland food for now. Of course, my grilled cheese sandwiches are made with a tasty combo of white cheddar and Swiss cheeses. None of that garbage wrapped in plastic for a healing woman."

Kim laughed and regretted it when the sharp pain sliced through her head. This concussion made her migraines look like mere paper cuts. After her vital signs were checked for the final time, she sat in the wheelchair provided by the aide and hoped she would be home soon. Her bed was calling her name. She had to sleep.

Kim was upset she'd forgotten about her conversation with Adele. A brain injury could affect her work. Did she need to seek supervision? She had a colleague who would do that for her. What about lost income? Of course, it was fitting that last month had been the first positive bank balance since she'd clawed out from the impact of Brad Newton's financial hit. And what about her commitment to the dog owners she worked for? Maybe the temporary helper she'd hired for later in May could start early. Her anxiety was spiraling, and she knew Adele was aware of her shallow breathing and sweaty palms. Sleep would help with her many concerns, and she looked forward to snuggling in her bed at home.

No such luck. As Adele helped her into the passenger seat of the 2008 Toyota that the older woman refused to trade, Dan Westbrook leaned over the door frame, brushing her hand with his. Her fingers tingled with his touch. This man held both menace and attraction, things she certainly didn't need to deal with right now.

"Good morning, ladies," Dan said. "I'm glad to see you're being discharged as planned, Dr. Newton. Mind if I stop by when you get home? It will save you a trip downtown."

Knowing this was not a request, Kim nodded.

"Your visit will have to be brief," Adele said. "Kim's got a terrific headache and is quite exhausted. As you should know, no real sleep occurs in a hospital."

"Understood," Dan replied. "It won't take long."

After a quick drive to Kim's cozy Broad Ripple home, Dan entered immediately after the women. Kim crossed her fingers that he wouldn't be here for any length of time. She was spent. In spite of her exhaustion, she was intrigued by the detective. He was dressed in the usual city detective fashion: jeans topped by a sport coat and button-down shirt. No tie, and instead of dress shoes, he wore running shoes that had seen more than a few miles. He was tall, broad shouldered, and had a face with lines reflecting the difficult job he held. The wrinkles worked for him, though. She imagined that when he smiled, his whole face would light up.

Kim doubted Detective Westbrook smiled much. In addition to his grizzly job, he seemed to have other areas of pain in his countenance. His expression was calm but revealed little. How did he manage to keep it together? From seeing the worst of human behavior each day to doing his best to give victims their just due, his dark brown eyes had seen a lot.

As had hers, she admitted. Her job often required her to relive ugly moments in her patients' pasts. She and the detective had that in common. The gratification she received when patients began to heal was what got her through the day. Maybe police work was similar. The satisfaction of catching the bad guy and ensuring justice had to be about the same.

Kim's assessment of Dan was missing whatever personal life he had. Was he married? Did he have a significant other? Judging from the detective's behavior with her, she guessed he was divorced. He had the guarded demeanor of a man who'd been let down by a woman. But maybe she was projecting. Her letdown by Brad Newton had jaded her to the point she refused to date since their divorce.

Her friend Candi constantly nagged her about her unwillingness to "put herself out there," as the tired phrase went. Her buddy used all the usual arguments. There were still good men to be found. She'd been unlucky, not stupid. She deserved the best life could offer. *Well, deserving and finding were two different things.*

Where would she meet a good man? Dating clients was forbidden, for obvious reasons. Online matching services had been terrible failures. Her only "hits" on those sites were men like Brad, who loved the idea of the imaginary big money she was earning. Her church was her happy place, but in terms of single men it held meager pickings. Most of the good men there were decades older and very happy with their wives of fifty years. Even her parents had tried to fix her up after the divorce. Again, each meeting was a dismal failure. A few dates with a chemical engineer were promising, until he revealed he planned to move to California and would have no time in his life for a long-distance relationship. Clearly, his appearance at their restaurant meal was motivated by pressure from her mom and the fact that he didn't cook. She was brought back to the present by the detective's voice.

"Betty Shields told me about your work in the ED, Dr. Newton," Dan began. "Very impressive. It's unfortunate you had to give it up. I'm interested in the man who stole your identity and sued for malpractice. Your ex-husband will also merit questioning."

After shaking her head, which she immediately regretted, Kim was astounded at what she was hearing. "Why are we talking about my ex? Brad Newton lives in Turks and Caicos now, thanks to his generous divorce settlement and my inept lawyer. There's no way he could or would hurt me. And Tom Adams? Last I heard, he was in prison thanks to all that is holy. You should be looking for Russ's enemies, not mine. The attacks happened in Russ's place, remember? I was an accidental victim. Wrong place, wrong time."

"We're looking at all possibilities," Dan said mildly. "My partner is interviewing your friend Russ. As you told me yesterday, he seems to have no enemies. But we'll be sure before we quit searching for them."

"Okay. My ex-husband, Brad, was never physically abusive, which is what you're fishing for. He just liked his cash unearned and preferably from me. Plus, you probably already know the man who tormented me last year has been incarcerated, for quite a while as a matter of fact. He couldn't be the person who hurt Russ and me."

"Yes, I did a detailed search after I talked to Betty. He got quite a long sentence, didn't he? Which leaves another important question."

"Which is?" Kim and Adele asked in unison.

"What else did he do to you, Dr. Newton?"

Dan observed Kim as she tried to hide her pain. This time it wasn't in her head, but her soul. Her face was in turn shocked, terrified, and then stoic. She was a pro at covering, likely due to her years of experience as a therapist. She'd given herself away, though. The memory of Adams's crime was still painful enough for her to crumble completely. A quick glance at Adele confirmed his thinking. The older woman was horrified and looking at Kim with true anguish. The number of tells in each woman's face was significant.

The possibilities raged through Dan's consciousness. Had Kim been beaten, raped, held hostage for days? Had

Adams manipulated her into feeling sorry for him so he could get close to her and exact retribution for his perceived humiliation in the ED?

Dan's conversation with Betty Shields rewound through his brain. She'd implied a lot more damage to Kim than just identity theft and a nuisance lawsuit. Betty had been sending him a message about Adams. It looked like Nurse Bossy was a better detective than he was.

Kim's beautiful face was the primary clue. Her blue eyes clouded and the skin around them crumpled. She didn't seem to be a woman who cried easily, but her eyes were filled to the brim. She began to hug the wrap Adele had placed over her shoulders. He was no psychologist, but it was obvious Kim Newton had lingering PTSD. What had that monster put her through?

As he'd anticipated, Adele took charge. "That's enough, Mr. Westbrook. You're tormenting my friend after I cautioned you not to. Please leave."

Dan was granted a temporary reprieve by a knock on the door. A woman about Kim's age let herself in and called, "Kim, where are you? Adele texted me and said we needed girl time to help you relax."

Candi Linderman was introduced as Kim's friend since their college sorority days. She gave Kim a gentle hug and eyed Dan carefully. "Who are you?" she asked, not a bit gently.

"I'm Detective Westbrook with the IMPD," Dan answered. "Just here to ask Dr. Newton a few questions."

Candi glanced at her friend huddled on the sofa. "Based on what Adele said and on what I see, Kim's in no shape to be interrogated," Candi announced. "Why don't you come back next week?"

Dan sighed. "Because next week the person who attacked Dr. Newton and Mr. Kellams will be long gone. Or, if the attacker is unhappy with being interrupted by Kim, he or she will be back to finish the job. That's why."

"That may be so," Adele said. "But Kim is still in bad shape. She needs the comfort of people who love her. Then she needs a long nap. As I said before, please leave, Detective."

Wow, being kicked out of Kim Newton's presence twice in twenty-four hours. And both times by older, formidable women. Plus, the friend from way back in Kim's college days. That had to be a record, three females telling him to get lost. Not a record he was particularly proud of.

"I understand, and I apologize to you all," he said. "I hope your recovery is smooth, Dr. Newton. We'll talk later in the week."

"I'll be screening her calls," Adele said. "So maybe you'll talk and maybe you won't."

That brought a smile to Kim's pale face. "It's all right, Adele. I'm confident by the end of the week I'll be able to assure Detective Westbrook that Tom Adams couldn't have had anything to do with this. Goodbye, Detective."

Those blue eyes were clear of tears now. This woman regrouped quickly. Tough wasn't the word to describe her. Never one to wordsmith his thoughts, Dan searched his brain anyway. *Resilient,* that was it. Kim Newton had endured a lot from men, but she marched on despite it all.

Kim rose and moved toward what he supposed was her bedroom. He had a sudden urge to follow and try to comfort her, soothe her. Maybe even ease into bed with her after all this was over. Which was ridiculous. She was a victim in an open case, not a friend or lover. He felt a sudden sense of loss at what he imagined her presence in his life could mean. He knew in his bones they could be good together. Not just in the sack, either. Kim could be the woman who would challenge him, excite him, and just be fun to be around.

He exited the house, followed closely by Adele and Candi. The door literally hit him in the backside as he stepped onto the small porch. Whatever her story, Kim Newton had strong, loyal friends.

He was also struck by the home itself. Dr. Newton had modest surroundings, maybe due to the divorce settlement she'd mentioned. The living room was nice enough, but years of experience in other people's homes told him the furnishings were far from new. She'd made the best of things after her split. He admired that. After his divorce, he'd bought out the display rooms at a couple of generic furniture stores, convinced it would ease his pain.

Kim, on the other hand, had put together a home (well, a living room, at least) that had charm without being untouchable. The blue plaid sofa had seen better years but was aided by a plush throw in a warm beige color. He had a similar blanket type thing the salesperson had added to his order for free, out of sympathy Dan had conjectured. The side chairs were solid blue, one being a leather recliner he instantly knew was comfortable. The scratches on the leather spoke of its second-hand origins. The room's walls were decorated with photos of Kim and an older couple, probably her parents. And over the sofa was some type of woven thing with long fringe, hanging from a wooden rod. Maybe Kim Newton was a closet hippie, her sensibilities hearkening back to the sixties.

Since he couldn't question Dr. Newton any longer, Dan went to the IMPD Northside office. He used the extensive FBI search program to review the trial of Tom Adams. Interestingly, the records had been sealed. Kim was listed as one of those who testified, as were the emergency department staff members, Tom's new therapist, and a few character witnesses. His gut twisted, a sign his guess had been correct. Tom Adams had done more than steal Kim's identity. The records were likely sealed because he'd sexually assaulted her.

It wasn't easy to seal records in Indiana but given Kim's profession, he understood the rationale. Being an assault victim wasn't something a therapist wanted a client to know right out of the gate. Sure, in some instances such a disclosure could be therapeutic but not via public record. Once again, he admired Kim's courage.

That would explain Adams's lengthy sentence. Identity theft had been the least of Kim's problems. No wonder she didn't do therapy in person anymore. Seeing patients via telehealth provided her a semblance of safety. How ironic she'd just been attacked while attempting to walk a friend's dog.

But he couldn't assume Tom Adams was the perpetrator this time. He was in prison, after all. It was time to check out Russ Kellams. Using the latest law enforcement search program revealed very little information about Russ. An easy Google search yielded more. As Kim reported, Russ was the recipient of several design awards. Most recently, he was named "The Most Innovative Decorator of the Year" by the local city magazine. A search of his LinkedIn profile again confirmed what Kim had told him. Russ was self-taught, a master with color *(what colors did a place need, other than brown and beige?)*, and well-liked in the community. Knowing there was always more to a person's life separate from their public persona, Dan looked at Russ's Facebook and Instagram pages.

Sure enough, there were plenty of snarky comments about Russ's design abilities. His style was compared to a first-grader's experiments with Crayola crayons, a gorilla throwing paint samples on the wall, and worse. Some were so full of vitriol that heat rose in Dan's chest. One comment went so far as to tell Russ to watch his back. Weren't social media platforms supposed to edit this garbage?

Further online digging allowed Dan to find several TikTok videos that parodied Russ's style. One woman gave her toddler jars of finger paint and encouraged him to "decorate" the shower walls. His partner Anson would have to check these clowns out.

Okay, Russ Kellams had enemies, no matter what Kim Newton believed. Professional jealousy was a powerful motivator for violence. Dan sent a quick email to his partner, hoping he was still meeting with Russ. This new information could be helpful.

Five minutes later, Anson Yeager turned the hallway corner and met Dan at his desk. "I just got your email, pal. Too bad I was already on the way here. Russ Kellams is conscious, but still pretty weak. He has no idea who would want to do him harm." Juggling his car keys and a large travel mug, Anson sipped his bitter coffee, heavy with cream and sugar, and added, "Of course, no one ever does."

"Read my email," Dan said. "We've got some folks to ask Russ about, believe me."

After a few minutes, Anson agreed. "These fancy design types sound like street thugs," he said. "What a collection of hate. The videos are low blows, too."

"Ah, be careful with your terminology my friend," Dan cautioned. "I've learned during my research that Russ wasn't a real designer, he was a *decorator*. Evidently there's a lot of difference in terms of education, certification, et cetera, et cetera. The thing is, Russ didn't have any of that, and his success was a sore spot for many people."

"So, Russ had jealous colleagues," Anson said. "Suddenly our suspect list is growing."

"Yeah, we might have to interview a handful of designers and their loved ones who have posted ugly comments. It's interesting that they used their real names when they commented. And they'll lead us to others, I'm sure."

Dan and Anson worked in their usual style, which was to overdose on caffeine while they brainstormed about possible suspects. After an hour of checking databases and online sites, they decided Russ Kellams had at least two enemies who merited questioning today. One last computer update led Anson to pound the desk.

"Patrick O'Laughlin, the guy who called Kellams a monkey with a paint can, is dead."

"What of?" Dan asked. Maybe they were on to a string of attacks, not just one.

"He had a massive coronary last week," Anson grumbled. "And based on what I'm reading in his obit, a significant history of heart disease. It doesn't feel like someone got to him." Anson listed the other possible suspects under the header "Professional Jealousy" and turned to Dan.

"I'll connect with most of these tomorrow," Anson said. "Who else should we talk to today?"

CHAPTER THREE

"THAT WOULD BE STEVE Knepper, Kellams's former partner. It takes a certain level of anger to post ugly things about someone you were in business with. Tell me more about that partnership."

"Like most professional matches, K&K Interiors started out great and ended badly," Anson said. "They had a grand opening party two years ago. It was attended by Indy's elite. Even the mayor showed, though based on what I'm reading, Mrs. Mayor was the reason. She loved Kellams's work. Knepper is frowning in all the photos of the three of them."

"It would seem we've got jealousy from day one. What about the finances?" Dan sipped his lukewarm coffee and grimaced.

"Not good, based on the bankruptcy they filed twenty-two months after the business started." Anson paused, read more on his computer screen, and continued. "This is interesting. Kellams paid back all the outstanding debts from the company. It took him until just a few weeks ago, but he did it."

"Okay. In addition to professional jealousy, do we now add financial envy? Do you think Knepper resented Kellams's ability to generate that much cash? Although it certainly helped Knepper's bottom line. He's got no debt and is free to build another business. It doesn't add up."

Dan looked out the grungy window. There had to be more to the story of K&K Interiors. "Prior to the bankruptcy, how was business? Were they twiddling their thumbs for almost two years, accumulating debt through advertising and schmoozing in the community?"

"Looks like they were busy," Anson said. "Come here and look at the photos on their old website. K&K completed over twenty projects in under two years."

The partners browsed through the pictures. They looked at each other and nodded. "Kellams did all the work," Dan said. "I see bright grade-school colors everywhere. Did Knepper do *any* of the decorating?" He drummed his fingers on the old desk. "Maybe he was the finance guy."

Anson moved to another computer screen. He pulled up a solo search on Steve Knepper. "Look at this, buddy. Knepper's stuff looks like my bachelor pad. Even I know this furniture is basic. My decor matches almost perfectly. And his favorite color palette seems to be beige on beige."

"Looks like my place, too," Dan said. For a reason he couldn't fathom, he flashed back to Kim's little house. He remembered it as a cozy study in blues. Light blue window shades, the slightly darker blue plaid sofa and mismatched chairs, and purply-blue flowered pillows. It felt like a home, not a place to snooze and eat. He knew Kim's décor reflected more than just her design sensibility. Creating a true home required love and devotion. Kim could be a woman overflowing with both.

Realizing again that under different conditions he would like to know Kim better, he wondered what she'd be like without this latest attack. Would she be condescending to a lowly IMPD detective? How would her profession impact her relationships? Would she be on the hunt for some sort of psychological flaw in those she met?

He doubted it. Betty, Adele, and Candi cared deeply for Kim. Her interactions with her friends were normal, absent of any deep analysis or probing. She just seemed like a good woman, albeit one with great looks. He sighed.

Startled by his thoughts, he had another sip of his noxious coffee. This woman was getting to him, even though he'd just met her. He reminded himself she was the "enemy," a member of the psych brigade that had been a part of the destruction of his marriage. He wondered what would have happened if he and Deb had seen a therapist like Kim. He'd probably still be divorced, since Deb was already seeing other men while they made their futile effort at marriage counseling.

Jerking himself back to the present, he added, "I sure wouldn't pay anyone to decorate like Knepper does. How in the world did these two get together and form a business?"

"Another mystery for us to solve," Anson said. "The financials will help us a lot. In the meantime, let's go visit

Steve Knepper. He's once again self-employed. His office is in Fountain Square, very trendy."

Having had enough coffee for a week, each man chugged a bottle of water while they drove in Dan's car to Steve Knepper's new office. Fountain Square was up-and-coming, the focus of several revitalization projects and home renovations. Dan noted Knepper's studio exterior which was appropriately worn and understated. And *beige,* with faux-aged signage covering the upper third of the storefront. How did this guy make a living?

They entered and were immediately greeted by a thin, silver-haired man. "How may I help you gentlemen?" he asked smoothly, as he studied their rumpled jackets.

Dan flashed his badge and answered, "Detective Westbrook, IMPD. This is my partner, Anson Yeager. Are you Steve Knepper?"

The smooth manner disappeared. "I am. What could you possibly want with me?"

"Your former partner was stabbed and nearly died yesterday," Anson said. "We're checking all friends and acquaintances for leads."

Apparently aware of the attack, Knepper nodded and regrouped. "I'm not sure I'm either a friend nor an acquaintance Russ would acknowledge," he said. "Russ and I are not speaking. If you've done any investigating at all, you're aware of our former partnership. It ended badly. Russ was determined to set the tone for our work. I was under the mistaken impression I would have equal input into our designs. And he was a terrible spendthrift."

Knepper paused and was quick to add, "But I'm truly sorry about the attack on Russ. When I heard about it on the news, I called his housekeeper. She said he was going to make it, thank goodness." Looking around at his empty showroom, he nodded to a young woman at the design station. "We'll be in the back, Andie."

Knepper waved them into his office, reminding his young female assistant to alert him for any phone calls. After they were seated, he continued. "Why don't you ask me what you need to know? No reason for me to tell you things you've deduced for yourselves."

Dan shifted in his chair. Steve Knepper was both angry at and concerned for Russ Kellams. He wanted to know why. "First off, where were you yesterday around noon?"

"I was here, and since I helped one very particular customer from around eleven to one-thirty, I have an alibi. Satisfied?"

"Good, we'll check that out after you give us the name and contact information for that person." Dan eyed Knepper, who looked calm. "And yes, we know about the bankruptcy and about Russ paying all the claims against the business. What happened?"

"I just told you. Russ was a spender, which is fine if you're able to generate an accurate project estimate and allow for profit." Knepper ran his hands through his hair, taking obvious care not to muss it too much. "He'd lowball potential clients, then run through the budget before he was halfway finished with the job. It was a nightmare."

As usual, Anson decided to use his considerable skills at playing good cop. "Sounds like a frustrating situation, especially for a designer with ideas of your own. How did you handle it? Didn't you tell him how you felt?"

"I handled it every way I could think of," Knepper said, shaking his head. "I cajoled, argued, and had our accountant in on a few meetings. All that. Nothing worked. Russ insisted once we had a 'presence' in Indianapolis, we'd charge more for our work. The presence never came, or at least it never satisfied Russ. Creditors tend to be impatient about that sort of thing."

"So that's why Russ paid everyone off?" Dan asked.

"That's why. I refused to take on what was essentially Russ's debt." After this announcement, Knepper's face ran the gamut from anger to sorrow. To Dan's surprise, the man was tearful. He glanced at Anson, who picked up the cue.

"Steve, that's awful. Man, I feel for you. But you seem to have landed on your feet here in Fountain Square. How's business?"

Rolling his eyes, Knepper gestured to the outer showroom. "It's building. Slow going, except for the few television shows I've been able to provide staging items for."

Taking a sip from what looked to be a hand-crafted coffee mug, he said, "Good thing I have an antiquing side business. The entertainment industry is currently hot for mid-century modern accessories. Indiana is the place to pick those up cheap. My weekends are spent picking." He looked away and continued. "Russ and I used to have the best time picking at flea markets and yard sales." He drummed his fingers on the desk, then regrouped. "My earthy minimalist style is coming back. But it's slow, as I said."

Dan was pleased to hear his own decor had a name. *Earthy minimalist* sounded a whole lot better than *beige and light beige*. Anson also looked pleased. But back to the work at hand.

"Steve, other than you, who do you think would hate Russ enough to try to kill him?"

"What?" Knepper stood, turning over his chair in the process. "You can't be serious. Russ and I had a falling out, but there's no way I could kill anyone. Even you pointed out he paid off all our bills. Why would I want to hurt him?" Tears formed again in his eyes. "I could never hurt Russ," he said softly.

Andie, purple-haired and about twenty-five, stood in the office doorway. "Mr. Knepper, there's a customer who needs your help." Whispering, she added, "He's gutted his home on Lexington Avenue and needs your input with his design. I think he's one of those guys who thought he could put the place together on his own. He said he just came back from IKEA and couldn't believe everything had to be assembled. Who doesn't know that?" A dramatic eye roll finished her announcement.

Regaining his composure, Knepper moved to the showroom. "Gentlemen, I have work to do. Please contact me if you have other questions. And if you see Russ, tell him I'm praying for him to heal quickly." Before he left, Anson obtained the name and contact information of the client Knepper said he was helping at the time of the attack.

Dan decided to make the most of the visit. Studying the woman's name badge he asked, "Miss Thompson, the IMPD needs your help. Do you have a minute?"

"Sure. Call me Andie. I'll need to answer the phone, but just between us, it doesn't ring much. What's up, Officer?"

After introductions were made, Dan decided to be blunt. Anson could ease the path if he got too brusque with the woman who provided the only color in the showroom. "Did you know Russ Kellams?"

"I've met him a few times, mostly when he'd come in and argue with Steve. It broke my heart because they were besties before K&K went under."

"Besties?"

"Yeah, they went to college together and were in each other's weddings. Mr. Knepper has all the design credentials, but I think Mr. Kellams just picked things up on his own. They were so pumped about starting their business. It's so, so sad how it all turned out."

"That's just awful," Anson said, oozing with sympathy. "What do you think happened?"

"From what I could tell, Mr. Kellams was one of those designers who would never cut corners. Even when a client had something she wanted to keep, like a chair of Grandma's or whatever, Russ would say no. His design had to flow." Andie shrugged.

"That's tough. Must have been hard on you to witness all that," Anson said. "And it put you in the middle of a conflict between two good guys." Nodding, Andie offered Anson a tentative smile.

Having had enough of Anson's syrupy routine, Dan asked, "How bad were the arguments?"

"Not that bad. I've had worse with my mom, and *way* worse with my boyfriend. Mostly it was the same each time. Russ would tell Steve to pay his share of the bills and Steve would answer he'd paid his part by generating leads for most of their contracts. Russ would fume and then Steve would remind him the project estimates were always way low."

"Did that sound right to you?"

Andie hesitated. Anson said, "It's okay, Andie. We're just collecting background information. Mr. Kellams was attacked, and we need to find the scum who would do such a thing."

Comforted, Andie said, "It made sense to me. Steve told me lots about their business. Russ is an innovative decorator, but terrible with money. It's odd though. Every time Steve talks about Russ, he tears up. Believe me, he's not a waterworks kind of guy. He really cares for Russ. Like I said, they have a lot of history."

"Thanks, Andie. You've been a great help to us," Anson said. "We'll let you get back to work, but please give me a call if anything else comes to mind that could aid in the investigation." He handed her a card, included his handwritten personal cell phone number, and they left Knepper's world of beige.

Dan and Anson walked to their car. "What do you think?" Dan asked.

"I think Knepper's off our suspect list," Anson replied. "He made a good point about not having any lingering animosity toward Russ because he paid off the creditors."

"The waterworks, as Andie put it, looked real to you?"

"They did. I think the busted partnership was a real loss for him."

Dan wasn't so sure, but Anson had a point. Did Knepper have a legitimate motive to kill his former partner? They would come back and talk to him later if his alibi didn't authenticate.

After a quick stop for a late lunch, the pair headed back toward the office. Dan's phone rang, and he continued to drive while the call paired with his car's audio. "Detective Westbrook?"

"Speaking," Dan said. "Who's this?"

"It's Steve Knepper. You were just here forty-five minutes ago. I thought of something after you left. The client I needed to help had just gone through a rough divorce."

"Okay. I fail to see what this has to do with Russ Kellams," Dan groused.

"Yes, well. I think Russ's ex-wife might be worth talking to. When he was determined to pay off the bankruptcy bills, they were still married. Alana was angry that Russ didn't just let the bills stay unpaid or put the squeeze on me. By taking responsibility, Russ was hampering her lifestyle, not to mention that of their son. When all was said and done, they were divorced."

Knepper took a breath. "Not the worst divorce I've seen, but not the best. In my opinion, that marriage had a quick expiration date anyway. Alana is high maintenance, if you get my drift, and she has a fiery temper. She can be sweet sometimes, but Russ finally realized her true nature when she pitched a fit about the bankruptcy payoff. Last I heard she'd hooked up with a pro athlete. That would be more her style than a decorator hustling for business. Not having Russ's money and cachet moved things along for Alana."

"Thanks, Steve," Anson said, as he listened to the conversation. "We appreciate this information."

After ending the call, Dan said, "Let's get back to the office and do a search on Alana Kellams. And we should ask Russ about her."

Something didn't add up, though. Kim had said she was sure she heard a male voice when she was attacked. Stabbing Russ and then knocking Kim out required significant strength. Sure, voices could be disguised, and some women were strong and knew how to use leverage when attacking someone bigger, but Dan didn't buy in. Not yet. They needed to assess Alana Kellams, both for anger and physicality. And for the presence of a tough new lover who may have been in on the attack.

The thought of judging a woman's strength brought Kim Newton to mind. He wondered how she was doing.

Should he check on her again? Her old lady neighbor and the sorority pal were probably doing a good job taking care of her, but Dan was worried. Something about Kim stuck with him. She was brave, smart, and hard-working, but also vulnerable. He wanted to protect her, which was totally out of bounds.

The small gold cross around her neck had also caught his attention. Evidently, she was a psych type, *and* she might be a religious zealot. What a great combination. If she couldn't analyze her patients into submission, she'd guilt them to making the changes they needed in their lives. All the while preaching and scolding.

He knew he was being totally unfair. Nothing about Kim Newton screamed guilt-inducing or wanting others to submit to her will. She seemed like a perfectly nice woman, one who was trying to make her way in the world after a couple of awful experiences with men. He could show her what a good guy could be like. His gut told him again they'd be good together.

What was wrong with him? He needed to focus.

He and Anson arrived at the office determined to find a credible lead. A quick search on Alana Kellams yielded some interesting tidbits. She was the mayor's sister-in-law, which explained Mr. and Mrs. Mayor's presence at the K&K grand opening. Though recently divorced from Russ, she was already engaged to an Indiana Pacer second-string guard. They had a waterfront house on Geist Reservoir, and she was pregnant with their child, due in July. This made Alana less likely to be the attacker, but her new fiancé had plenty of strength and muscle. Whose baby was Alana carrying? Would the answer to that question provide a motive for murder?

The story of Russ Kellams's divorce twisted Dan's gut. He'd bet the farm that Alana Kellams had wanted Russ to be more "emotionally available." Poor guy was trying to keep his business afloat while she was hell-bent on keeping up with her sister's prestigious lifestyle.

"Typical," he said aloud.

"What?" Anson asked.

"This Alana person. I've got her pegged."

Anson studied him across the front seat. "No, if anything you've got her pegged as your ex. Be careful, buddy. You think you've over your split, but you're not."

"Maybe."

"And watch yourself with Dr. Newton," Anson added. "You look at her like she's the ideal woman. No crushing on victims, okay?"

"*Crushing?* You in seventh grade, Anson? No crushing going on here."

CHAPTER FOUR

CANDI AND KIM TALKED for just under an hour. They laughed over their sorority antics, Kim cooed over Candi's latest photos of her daughter, and ate a hearty lunch together. Her friend's presence had the effect Adele had hoped for. Kim relaxed a little and was able to remember fun, carefree times.

"Here you are, comforting me when you've had a huge loss yourself," Kim said as they finished lunch. "How are *you* doing?"

Candi set her face, as if determined not to cry in front of her bruised and battered friend. "I'm good, Kim. Derrick's been gone almost two years now. Natalie doesn't remember him at all, which is both comforting and sad for me. I'm blessed to have the support of my family and his, so there's lots to be grateful for. God has been my rock, as you know."

Kim remembered the horrific car accident in which Derrick Linderman had been killed. A terrible storm had flooded parts of the interstate and a careless driver had been going way too fast as he hydroplaned into Derrick's car, causing it to leave the highway, flip, and hit a tree.

Because the driver's BAC had registered as terribly drunk, way over the state's legal alcohol limit, Candi and her daughter had won a sizeable settlement from his insurance company. The medical staff assured her Derrick ended life with no pain. But she was still alone to raise Natalie, her precocious three-year-old daughter. Candi's faith had gotten her through the hell on earth she'd been subjected to after Derrick's death. In fact, her friend's unwavering belief had helped Kim connect with God in a way she never had.

"Gratitude," Kim said, nodding. "That's what I have to work on. Thanks for reminding me. My life is good, I have healthy parents and good friends, and a career I love. Thanks for the reminder, pal," she repeated.

"And you've just met a great looking detective," Candi added. "What's his story? I gave him a hard time because you're obviously spent, but he has potential."

"No, he doesn't," Kim answered. "He's working Russ's case. Period. I'll admit he's a fine man but be aware of his edgy tone. He's focused on one thing, and that's finding whoever attacked Russ and me. My sense is that edge transfers to all areas of his life. Not something I need now, or ever."

"Edge or dedication?" Candi asked. "In my opinion, he needs to have that edge or he's not much of a detective."

"Either way, not something I need in my life."

Exhaling sharply, Candi looked at her best friend. "Listen, Kim. Since you're concussed and at my mercy, I'm going to tell it to you straight."

Kim's eyes widened. She smiled, knowing Candi was the sweetest woman in the world, and therefore didn't really want to have Kim at her mercy. "Okay, I'm ready for your straight talk. Let me have it."

"It's time for you to be interested in men who have a little more maturity, more seasoning. Men who could let you be independent but also take care of you if the situation warranted. And men who would let you take care of them if they were in need."

"Brad certainly let me take care of him," Kim said. "Is that what you're suggesting?"

"No, you missed the other part of my deep thinking. You need a man who could take care of you instead of leaching off you constantly. Dan Westbrook strikes me as a guy strong enough to take care of himself. And you. But I sense there's also a part of him that wishes for a woman strong enough to tend to him when he's down or low." Candi scowled. "Brad Newton could never take care of himself. Even with your big bag o'money, he's still bartending, and only when the urge strikes him. Such a loser."

"Aren't you supposed to be making me feel better?"

"Yes, and I'm also supposed to be your friend who slaps you up the side of the head when you're ignoring the good right in front of you. Knocking you around is impractical right now, given your concussion, but you get my point." They both laughed and Candi hugged Kim as she rose to leave. "Look, Brad fooled me, too. I'm not implying you were at fault for trusting him. We all get a romance mulligan or two. But Dan looks like he could be the real deal. Don't write him off."

Kim hugged her friend back. "Thanks, Candi. I'll give your wise words some thought. But you need to remember Dan is a detective working a case, not a romantic guy on a singles site."

"Fair enough," Candi said. As she left, Adele offered her some freshly baked cookies for Natalie, which she accepted readily. "Love you, Kim," she said as the front door closed.

Candi went home to relieve the babysitter she'd hastily contacted after Adele's call. Adele finally left for a few hours after Kim's repeated assurances that she would be fine for the rest of the afternoon and evening. Relishing her privacy after a harrowing twenty-four hours of chaos, Kim made a cup of tea. Despite her friends' efforts, relaxing was impossible. Instead of praying for Russ's recovery, her mind's eye wouldn't let go of Tom Adams's face, which made no sense.

A handsome face, no doubt. But a face hiding untold secrets and hidden cruelty. She'd gotten through the horror with God's unending help. God had also given her physical strength, strength enough to disable Tom before he could do anything else to her. Half-naked and groggy from whatever he'd forced her to drink, she was able to connect the pointy toe of her high heel to Tom's groin.

She fled, wrapping a quilt around her shoulders and running to Adele's house.

It all began when Tom arrived at her front door, seemingly earnest in his desire to convince her he hadn't been playing games or seeking drugs the night before in the emergency department. Before she could send him away, he'd barged in, sucker-punched her, and dragged her into the kitchen. After he made her drink from his water bottle, he ranted for several minutes about the need for women to remain where they belonged, at home and always available to meet their husbands' needs. He also detailed his plan to steal her identity, which had already begun thanks to his hacking skills.

Oddly, he was calm for the most part, emphasizing that Kim should be punished for embarrassing him in front of the hospital staff. Surely, she could understand that such a transgression must be paid for. She had nearly vomited when he began to undress her.

Fighting her dizziness and pain, Kim had tried to focus and respond to his irrational venting, which she knew immediately was a mistake. After Tom's subsequent punches, she was about to black out when she kicked him hard where it counted. God was with her, and she was forever thankful. She wondered about the theology of thinking that God liked hurting anyone, but nonetheless, she was grateful she'd found the strength to disable Adams.

Willing the nightmare away, Kim forced herself to stay in the present. She was safe, her credit was cleared, and Tom Adams was in jail. More immediately, Russ was going to recover. God was good, once again. If only she could rid herself of the interrupted sleep, constant looking over her shoulder, and fear of life in general. It will come, she told herself. With God's help and love, peace will come. Unfortunately, this latest attack on Russ had caused the old trauma to return in full force.

She recalled her favorite childhood Bible verses, the ones telling her to be still, that she could handle anything with Christ's help, and that the just would prevail. The sacred words rang hollow today. Justice seemed so elusive. Even Adams's prison sentence had been less time than the prosecutor had asked for, based on his ability to charm the court-appointed psychologist who had assessed him. And he'd sued her for malpractice from jail, thanks to a scummy local lawyer who lived for publicity. Shuddering, she remembered to give everything to God, but it was hard.

Trust, she told herself. How many times had Jesus proven to be trustworthy? Lots of times. As a kid, her path had been smooth, and her education paid for by her loving parents. Maybe that easy upbringing had blinded her to Brad's charm.

Fundamentally, he was a good man, but a weak one. After her years of schooling, he wanted the good life. And he wanted her around, not working evenings which was when most of her clients were able to meet. His weakness had led him to seek other avenues for female companionship. At first, she was silly enough to believe his excuses and lies. Even catching him at dinner with another woman was explained away by Brad as a work-related meeting. But when she realized the credit card charges amounted to more than just dinners, she knew.

Those two years, one pre- and one post-divorce, had been a nightmare, perhaps a preview to the hellish night with Tom Adams. At first Brad seemed conciliatory in the divorce negotiations. They would split things evenly, which was a blessing for Kim since they had little. Later, though, he demanded a large portion of her first three years' earnings as a licensed psychologist, claiming he'd been her primary financial support during grad school. Those lean three years had almost crushed her faith, but God had held her in His arms. Her practice had grown after Brad's hold on her income expired and she was able to buy a home without any help from her parents. She thanked God for His constancy and for His gift of strength. Life had been good again, until her meeting with Tom in the ED.

Now she was back to building her trust in God. The PTSD was agonizing. Adele and Candi were her main supports. Her parents didn't know much about what had happened with Adams, since they had retired to Florida in the midst of all the trauma. She'd simply told them a problem client had been a nuisance, but that all was well now. Adele thought they should have been informed of Kim's pain, but she disagreed. At Adele's urging, she'd told Candi about what happened, and her friend had come through. Kim was blessed to have two good women on her side.

Candi had soothed her, confronted her, and let her cry when that was all Kim could do. Somehow her friend planted seeds of hope, the belief that there were good men in the world. Not that Kim wanted another man. After enduring Brad Newton and Tom Adams, Kim figured God meant for her to be single. Weren't there some psychological studies showing women were happier single? She was sure it was true in her case.

Somehow, the entry of Detective Westbrook into her life made it easier to trust God when she woke from her nightmares. Odd, but true. She'd take Dan's indirect comfort for now, though he had a way of sensing what she tried to keep hidden. He'd known instantly that Tom Adams had attacked her both physically and mentally. She guessed Westbrook was good at his job. Again, she'd take that comforting knowledge for now.

- - - - - - - - - - - - - -

Dan and Anson were at the entry to Alana Kellams's massive home on the water's edge at Geist. Having been warned of their visit, Alana met them at the door. She was beautiful, worthy of a magazine cover. Raven hair, striking green eyes, and olive skin tanned to perfection. Plus, a rounded belly. She was clad in the latest maternity fashion, which hugged her figure and emphasized how close she was to delivering her baby.

"Hello, gentleman," she said. "I'm worried. You were so vague when you called. Whatever can you want with me?" Her concern seemed genuine, and since her pregnancy was in its later stages, the woman could not have stabbed her ex-husband without help.

Dan glanced at Anson. Could it be possible Alana hadn't heard about Russ?

"We're here to check in about the attack on Russ Kellams," Dan said.

Alana stumbled and sat hard on a bench in the artfully decorated entryway. "What attack?" she whispered.

Jumping in as the sympathetic fellow he enjoyed pretending to be, Anson said, "We're sure sorry to tell you this way, Mrs. Kellams. Russ will recover, but his attacker is at large. Anything you can share will be helpful. Are you okay?"

Dan made silent gagging sounds in his head. Anson was a pro. No wonder he wasn't married. False charm came too easily to him. Every time he had a good woman in his life, he sabotaged it with a meaningless flirtation with someone else. His partner seemed to have a fear of commitment which led him to derail his relationships.

Great, now he was thinking like a marriage manual. Time to focus. He looked at Alana Kellams and focused in as she responded to Anson's sweet query.

"I'm fine, and I have no idea what has happened to Russ. My husband and I just returned from Las Vegas. I'm not Mrs. Kellams anymore, I'm Mrs. Smithson. Mrs. Clark Smithson. Tell me about Russ. He's still dear to me. Is he in the hospital? Can I see him?" Alana began deep breathing in an apparent effort to comfort herself.

After explaining yesterday's events and helping her to leave the entry, Dan sat opposite Alana in her enormous living room, highlighted by floor-to-ceiling windows. He noted it was decorated in light blue, with accents pieces in brown and beige. His beige-on-beige style was fundamentally sound but just needed a little help, he thought. Kim's living room had some blue furnishings, so maybe she could help him jazz up his place. He massaged his temples and forced himself to focus on Alana Smithson.

Anson brought Alana a glass of ice water from the massive kitchen. "We're looking for leads, Mrs. Smithson. Can you tell us why you and Russ divorced?"

The woman's eyes filled. "I'm pregnant, as you can obviously see. But Russ and I couldn't have any more kids after our son. I kept miscarrying. The doctors said it was his 'fault' though I hated that word. Who knows about secondary fertility issues? Maybe our body chemistries just didn't work well together. It could have been my fault as well as his. Anyway, he kept focusing on his business to avoid the pain. At least that's what I told myself. I never could figure out what was in that silly man's head." She brushed her cheeks with her perfectly manicured fingers and said, "I was alone with our son most days. Russ would come in after midnight and leave for the design studio before six. Our divorce was as amicable as a divorce can be."

She smiled and added, "I realize *amicable* is an overused word these days, but it was true in our case. In fact, when he found out I was pregnant this time, he sent flowers and offered to decorate the nursery."

Anson used his usual ingratiating tone and said, "I really hate to ask this, Mrs. Smithson. We heard from a source that you resented Russ's assumption of all the debt from K&K. Was that a contributing factor to your divorce?"

Alana sneered. "Knepper said that, didn't he? He's such a snake. Always resentful of Russ's talent, unwilling to branch out beyond his own 'sand and mud' style of decorating, and jealous that Russ and I had a good marriage."

She cradled her belly while she thought. "Anyway, I'll be honest. I *was* resentful of all the money Russ spent on the firm's debts. We were trying to have another baby and infertility treatments cost a lot. His insurance was terrible, so we shouldered that burden by ourselves. At the same time, I admired Russ's commitment to his clients and creditors. He explained that to leave all those unpaid bills would tarnish his reputation forever. Steve wasn't smart enough to understand that."

More follow-up questions yielded nothing of import. Alana's new husband did indeed play for the Pacers. They met at a charity function. Russ sent a bridal shower gift two months ago; a tasteful tea set Alana had registered for at Saks. He'd even come for dinner a few nights before she and Clark flew to Las Vegas to marry. Their son was close to both men. Relations between all of them were just peachy, as Anson noted. More to the point, the Smithsons had perfect alibis. Clark was at the blackjack table and Alana was shopping, having used her credit card several times in Vegas yesterday morning.

"I'm done for the day," Anson groused as he slumped in the car outside of the Smithson mansion. "All of our sure-fire leads cry when they hear about the attack on their fine friend Russ. Normally I'd say that was suspicious, but they seem real when they talk about him. What are we missing?

CHAPTER FIVE

KIM STIRRED AS THE sun peeped through the sheers covering her bedroom window. She wondered if she'd slept more than a half hour total for the night. She knew PTSD was no match for God's power, and she was continuing in her own therapy for the condition, but progress was slow. Until Tom's attack, Kim had been able to sleep anywhere, anytime. She was even a master of the quick nap.

Looking at her reflection as she brushed her teeth, she realized things had to change. Her eyes were red and cushioned with dark, puffy bags. Not to mention the bruising which nearly covered her whole face. Concealer would be her friend again today, especially if she left the house. She blew out a frustrated sigh. Tom still had power over her. His torture was embedded in her psyche which was understandable, but she was sick of it. It was time to reclaim her own power.

The irony was that she had used those very words with her own clients many times over the course of her career. She shuddered as the stark reality hit her. Taking back her own power also meant she had to admit she could survive if it all happened again. If not with Tom, then someone else. Or something else, something unexpected and horrible. Life was too random, and human nature too flawed to assume there was true safety in this world. Only God held her safety and would provide her strength through whatever the future held. With God's help, she would survive, and even thrive.

A fragile sense of peace settled over her, interrupted by the ringing of her cell phone. She was surprised to see Russ's ex-wife's information on the caller ID. Kim and Alana were cordial, but not friends. Maybe Alana wanted to check in on Kim's injuries.

"Hi, Alana. What's up?" Kim asked.

"Hi, honey. How are you doing?" Alana spoke in a rush, barely pausing between sentences. "The police guys came by yesterday and filled me in about you and Russ being attacked. Then a few minutes ago, Russ called. He needs a ride home from the hospital. Can you go with me?"

Taking a second to process Alana's request, Kim said, "Sure, if you need me, I'm there."

"It's just that I'm so huge with the baby, Kim. I can drive but I'll need help getting Russ into the car and carrying all his things. And he said he's got a room full of flowers he wants us to drop off at his mom's assisted living facility. Are you able to help with that? He'd love to see you." As if she suddenly remembered Kim had also been attacked, Alana added, "But only if you're able."

"Absolutely," Kim said, putting a cool washcloth over her face. The doctor said to take it easy for a week, but this wouldn't be strenuous work. And she wanted to see Russ. "Pick me up when you can, Alana. I'll be here."

Kim called Adele and filled her in on the plans for the morning. It was no shock that Adele disapproved. "You have no business being out and about, young lady. You're still healing yourself. From a *concussion*. Those doctors should have kept you in the hospital."

Knowing the futility of arguing, Kim used a different tactic. "Adele, you're probably right. I just want to see Russ with my own eyes, you know? And Alana will do all the driving. It will be fine."

"I give up with you young people," Adele said, forgetting Kim was thirty-six. "No one can tell you anything. I'll make you lunch, though. You and Alana can eat here when you're done with Russ. I've got a taco casserole ready to put in the oven."

Though she was sympathetic to Alana's probable lack of tolerance for spicy food this late in her pregnancy, Kim decided again not to argue. "That's really nice of you, Adele. I'll call when we're on our way back." She would tell Alana about the menu and let her decide if she wanted to pick up a sandwich on the way to Adele's.

Thirty minutes later, after a serious makeup session to cover her discolored face, Kim climbed into Alana's massive SUV. Alana looked at her wide-eyed. "Kim, I never should have called you," Alana said. "You look like death warmed over. I'm so sorry." So much for her efforts with concealer and blush.

Twenty minutes after that, they were in Russ's room. "Thanks be to heaven you're both here," he said, giving each a side hug. "I can't truly embrace you ladies but know it's in my heart."

Kim kissed Russ on the cheek, and both began to cry. "Russ, I had to see you for myself. I feel better now." In fact, Russ looked better than she did.

"Same here, sweetheart," he said, swallowing hard several times. "You've been through a lot, too. What a nightmare. Who would do this to us? Those cops have asked me everything except where I've hidden my mother's pearls. I have no clue, and unfortunately, neither do they."

"Really, Russ?" Alana asked. "I remember a few clients who were terrible to you after their designs were finished. You did everything to their specifications, but they wanted to wiggle out of paying you." Rubbing her belly, Alana added, "When you threatened to take them to a collection agency, things got pretty heated."

"No, those nice folks are my best supporters now," Russ said. "It helped that I talked to a couple of minor decorating magazines, and their homes were featured in an issue entitled, 'Midwest Chic.' Funny, huh?" He sat in the wheelchair offered by the aide and they made their way to the discharge area. Alane retrieved her car and soon Russ was settled in the front seat.

Alana looked at Kim, who was busy placing Russ's bag of hospital stash (toothbrush, deodorant, socks with grippy soles) in the hatchback area. "Those nasty fools weren't really funny, Russ. I'm sure Kim would say that those 'nice folks' should be investigated by Detective Westbrook."

"It wouldn't hurt, Russ," Kim said. "Since we're all flying blind here, I think the police should be informed of any possible leads."

"Okay, I'll tell that Anson fellow. He's coming to my place tomorrow to ask even more questions. I can't wait."

After giving Russ the bottle of water provided by the hospital, Alana and Kim loaded the car with several bouquets and planters. "My, you have a lot of admirers," Alana teased.

"Yes, the largest arrangement was from Steve," Russ said.

"Snake," Alana sneered.

"Now, now. No sense in picking at old wounds, honey. The K&K partnership is dissolved, just like our marriage. But we can still be friends, right?"

"That's not the same, and you know it," Alana sputtered. "We still love each other in our own way. Steve Knepper loves no one."

"Not true," Russ answered. "We may not be friends anymore, but he checked up on me after he heard about the attack."

Kim jumped into the chatter before Alana could argue further. "From my perspective, you two in the front seat have no business raising your blood pressures over such nonsense. We're all here, alive and kicking. That's what matters."

Everyone laughed. The drive to the assisted living facility took under ten minutes. The director came out to the car with a few employees pushing carts, and the flowers were delivered without any of the car's occupants needing to help.

"That's a break," Russ said. "I can barely move, Alana's 'great with child' as they used to say, and Kim still has bruising, stitches, and a big knot on her head. That director is all flash and phony smiles most of the time, but today he helped us and I'm grateful."

"Yeah, you're a grateful guy," Alana said. "All that gratitude stuff blinds you to people's true nature. Right, Kim?"

Kim didn't want to reopen Alana's tirade, since her head was starting to throb. She'd forgotten how testy Alana could get when Russ was in one of his Pollyanna phases. "People are people, Alana. Some better than others, as I well know. Let's just get to the job at hand which is to get Russ home safely."

Alana snorted her disagreement and asked, "Where to next? Do you want us to pick up some food for lunch? Make a grocery run? Go to the pharmacy? Tend to Reed?"

It took Russ a few seconds to process Alana's onslaught of questions. "My groceries are being delivered this afternoon. Reed is boarding at his favorite place until I can handle him. I've got the makings for a quick lunch, not that I'm hungry. I'll be fine with soup and half a sandwich. Get me home, ladies."

As Alana turned into Russ's development, an old, rusty red truck barreled out of nowhere and rammed the side of the SUV. The front seat, containing Alana and Russ, avoided the impact, but the rear of Alana's vehicle took the brunt of the force. Kim's tender head was jerked back and sideways before she hit the back-side door hard and landed on the spacious floor, sliding under the seatbelt she'd carefully fastened.

A car stopped at the condo entrance road and its driver came to help. "I saw it all," the man said. "That truck took aim; this was no accident. And where is it?"

The truck was long gone. The driver of the car, Paul, dialed 911 and within a few minutes an ambulance arrived. Histories were obtained. Russ and Alana were deemed fine to proceed to Russ's home, but Kim was semiconscious and placed into the ambulance for an ED evaluation.

Why did bad things keep happening to Russ? Kim wondered through her foggy consciousness. Closing her eyes, she took several deep breaths. The EMT attempted to soothe her, noting her vitals were good.

"You're going to be fine," he said, as he studied Kim's bruised face. "We'll get you checked out and you'll probably be on your way. Unless they want to keep you for observation, that is."

"Surely not," Kim mumbled. "There's no reason to stay in the hospital, is there?"

Shaking his head, the EMT replied, "Based on what your friends told us, you've had a recent concussion, so there might be. You've got to respect your brain, Ma'am. It could need some extended rest."

Terrific, Kim thought. *Two consecutive nights in my own bed must be too much to ask. Dear Lord, come to my aid, please. If this is about my lack of faith, I'm sorry. I trust You with all my being. Really, I do. But I could use a break and so could Russ.*

Three hours later, Adele appeared in the doorway of Kim's emergency department room. "As usual, these folks couldn't hit water if they fell out of a boat," she complained. "The hospital is on something called diversion, so they need beds for really sick people. As if your injuries don't count."

Kim smiled at Adele's fury. "I'd rather go home, Adele. Thanks for coming for me."

"I'm not only bringing you home, I'm going to live with you for the next week. You will be going nowhere, hear?" Adele commanded. "I promised I'd watch you carefully."

"You don't have to do that!" Kim said, grabbing her head with regret the instant the words were out. "I can manage fine, and you can call me a few times each day."

"Nope, they made me promise. Kim, your only other alternative was to go to a rehab facility for a week. I knew you wouldn't want that."

"Rehab? Like a nursing home?"

"Whatever it's called, you and your rattled brain need constant care and observation," Adele said. "I can provide that better than some institution."

"Yes, you can, dear friend. I owe you big. We'll turn it into summer camp, just the two of us."

Adele tsked in disapproval. "Sure, we'll have lots of fun, Kim. Mostly I'll be doing my crosswords and watching my soaps while you sleep. I also plan to bring Sam's old rifle over while we bunk together. No sense in being unprepared for whatever comes next."

Sam was Adele's deceased husband. He'd fought the good fight against his heart disease but had died a few months ago. Prior to Adams's final incarceration and while he was in the local jail, Sam had walked the Broad Ripple streets and neighborhood park with his handgun clearly visible in its belt holster while he used his cane to smooth his gait. "Open carry, closed carry, who cares?" he'd said. "I'm an eighty-eight-year-old man who has rights, and I'll tell the police that if they try to stop me. If that no-good piece of trash shows his face anywhere near Kim's place, he's getting a warm hello from me."

Kim smiled at the memory of Sam's love and protection, misplaced as it was. Between his fierce Irish temper and passion for Adele and Kim, he was an unforgettable guy. "I don't think we'll need the gun, but if it makes you feel better bring it," she said to Adele.

"You bet I will," her friend countered. "You're vulnerable, Kim. Whether you like it or not, you need to be careful. Russ is a trouble magnet right now. Somehow your connection with him is making you magnetized as well."

At that moment, Dan entered the room. "Hello again, Dr. Newton. We've got to stop meeting like this."

Kim groaned. "Detective." There seemed to be no point to her fighting his presence, strangely soothing as it was. But why would he want to talk to her? Russ was the one who kept getting attacked.

That thought ignited her fears for her friend. "Is Russ okay? And how about Alana? She's pregnant, you know."

"They're both well. In the end, the EMTs decided to take Alana with them for an exam and ultrasound to be sure she and the baby were all right, and they are. Russ leads a charmed life. His stitches are intact, and he's settled in at home. Alana's husband is on the way to pick her up."

"Why aren't you talking to Russ?"

"My partner Anson is with him. Russ needed something to eat before he could give us a statement. He's already described the truck that hit Alana's vehicle. The other development resident who witnessed the accident gave us a partial description of the truck's driver." Dan paused, giving Kim his assessment stare.

"I know where this is going," Kim said. "I didn't see anything. I was in the back seat, talking away to Russ. After that I've got nothing."

"Then let's start again. Who could be this angry with Russ? We've checked his former partner, his ex-wife and her husband, all with no good results. I think you've known Russ long enough to think of someone else who'd be hostile, or envious, or just vengeful enough to want to harm him."

Adele gathered all five feet of her stooped height and said, "Look, Detective Hot Shot. You're badgering my patient. She's post-assault, post-auto accident, concussed, and exhausted. Her discharge papers are on the way and then she's under my care. I will not allow you in her home until tomorrow. Got it?"

Kim gave Dan a wan smile. "I'll think about your questions. But for now, I'm with Adele. I can't think and I've got the headache to beat all headaches. I need to sleep."

Dan left, giving Kim another of his cards. She'd have to save them and replenish his supply when Russ's attacker was caught. As promised, her discharge papers arrived, and Adele bundled her into her car a half hour later.

- - - - - - - - - - - - - -

Home sweet home. Kim nestled into her bed; her stomach filled with Adele's taco casserole. It had been surprisingly good, and the hearty fare reminded her she could still tolerate nourishing, interesting food. Maybe that meant she could tolerate a nourishing, interesting life as well. Maybe.

What about Russ's latest assailant? She tried to remember who Russ had complained about when he'd won the Indy magazine award. Hadn't there been someone who called him out about his designs? It was in the recesses of her mind – a comment on Russ's Facebook page saying Russ didn't deserve to live, much less to receive the award. Surely Dan and his partner had checked social media sites for suspects. She hoped he'd told the detective's partner about the clients who tried to get out of paying his fees as well.

Back to the business of a nourishing, interesting life. What would such a life look like for her? She loved her work, so that box was checked. She had meaningful friendships – check. Her parents were healthy, enjoying the fruits of their years of hard work and due to their relocation to Florida, provided her a free vacation spot each year – check. She knew what was missing, but she hated to admit it. Someone to share her life with. That box was definitely not checked. But it was all too scary. She'd loved and lost, been attacked when she least expected it, and couldn't risk any of it again.

She reminded herself that in addition to her parents, Adele and Sam had been blessed with a good marriage. They bickered constantly, at first causing Kim concern that one or both of them were suffering from depression or dementia. But no, their testiness with each other was their way of maintaining their independence and ne- gotiating the differences of daily life. When Sam died, Adele was bereft but pragmatic. "He was a loving man, and we were lucky to have each other for as long as we did," she'd said. "He even held on and died two days after our sixty-fifth anniversary. That's how he was. Tough but thoughtful in ways you couldn't put your finger on some- times. You'll find that, too. Just wait, Kim. There's a Sam out there for you, mark my words."

Kim's eyes were heavy. Detective Westbrook's face ap- peared in her haze. That face had seen some things, way worse things than she'd ever experienced. The face was kind and tough at the same time. She wished they'd meet under different circumstances. Maybe he could be her Sam. But Dan Westbrook saw her as a victim, and right now that was all she was to him.

CHAPTER SIX

AWAKENING WITH WHAT FELT like a new lease on life, Kim stretched gingerly in her bed. Ever present, Adele appeared at the bedroom door. "How does breakfast sound?" she asked as she eyed Kim carefully. "Are you up to some food?"

"I'm ravenous," Kim said, smiling at her friend. "Last night was just what the doctor ordered. Delicious food and deep, uninterrupted sleep."

"Don't get used to it," Adele said. "Your friend from IMPD has already called twice, asking when he could stop by. I told him never."

Kim laughed, noting her head didn't hurt quite as much as yesterday. "I'm sure that went over well, Adele. Better be careful with the police. They can jail you for resisting or obstructing or something."

"Humph. They can catch me first." Adele was elderly, but still spry. Kim knew she could give Dan a good run. She was also adept with pepper spray, having used it on an aggressive neighborhood dog. Daring the owners to report her, she'd threatened to report *them* to the police instead for walking the dog off leash in Broad Ripple Park, an area full of small children, plus one elderly woman. Yes, Adele could hold her own with just about anybody.

"As it stands, I have nothing to tell him, other than to look at Russ's social media accounts. I remember a vague threat after Russ won the award."

"He's already done all that," Adele retorted. "Detective Westbrook said the only good suspect died of a heart attack last week." Adele told Kim the name of the dead man. "Which means he's back to questioning you, unfortunately."

Realizing that was indeed the fellow whose name she'd been searching for last night, the one who'd left the ugly comment on Facebook, Kim's good mood took a hit. It was back to square one in the search for people who would want to harm Russ.

Another hit to her outlook came when her phone jingled as she was brushing her matted hair, avoiding the tender stitches. Brad's name was on the ID. Just what she needed, either a taunt or a fake message of sympathy for her recent troubles, from the man who had upended her life with the very definition of *conditional* love. I love you *if* you've got money, *if* you work what amounts to part-time hours, *if* you focus on me alone.

"What's up, Brad?" she asked, forcing herself to be pleasant.

"I needed to hear your voice," Brad said. "One of my friends from Indy messaged me and said Russ and his dog walker had been attacked. I figured that must have been you. You two were always tight, and you loved that goofy dog. Are you okay?"

Kim's chest tightened. Everything good about Brad rushed into her consciousness. His caring nature, his former sweet thoughtfulness. He'd been sweet just until the divorce, when it occurred to him he could make a killing on her future income.

"I'm fine," she lied. "Evidently someone is jealous of Russ's success. The police are working on it."

"Thank goodness," Brad said. "I still care for you, Kim. You know that, right?"

Her throat swelled. This man was still able to tap into her feelings, her regret about the loss of what they'd had. But if she were to stay sane, she couldn't let him in. She had to be tough. "It's hard to swallow, Brad. You took a chunk of my money for three years. You cheated on me repeatedly. I hate to think what could have happened if you *didn't* care for me."

"Kim, you know that's an imperfect summary of what happened. You forget all the late nights you spent with your cohort classmates, most of whom were men, and then later with your evening clients. I was lonely all by myself, wondering what you were doing without me. Even when you were home, there was nothing left for me. You were exhausted and 'out of words' as you put it. Shouldn't a wife be more than a tired, silent presence?"

"Shouldn't a husband be able to voice his unhappiness before he jumps into bed with another woman?" Kim asked. Her head was hurting again. Why did she continue to expect decency from Brad Newton? Why did she never learn the futility of arguing with him?

Heaving a dramatic sigh, he said, "We're not going to settle this now, Kim. This call is international and costing me a fortune. Not that you care. I'm glad you're okay." He ended the call, maintaining control as usual.

Kim knew Brad had a cheap international phone plan, and that he'd lied to her yet again. At heart, he was a small, petty man, but that realization did little to help her feelings of loss.

As she chewed her heavily buttered toast between bites of Adele's delicious cheese omelet, Kim forced herself to think positive thoughts. There were lots of good men in the world, there had to be. She reminded herself yet again that she had many happily married friends. Candi had been happy with her husband until he was killed in the accident. Her parents' marriage was strong despite their having dealt with her dad's cancer, her mother's alcoholic sister, and so much more. And Adele and Sam were happy until the very end. Unbidden, Dan Westbrook's face popped into her head.

He was very handsome, as Adele would say, but he also seemed intelligent and observant. Beyond those qualities, he had that edge, a hardness that probably came with the job. She had treated a few policemen during the course of her career. When it came down to it, they were each unique individuals, but they all carried a heavy burden. Sometimes the pressures of the job also played havoc with their marriages. She said a quick prayer for Dan, that he would be successful in finding Russ's attacker and have peace in his personal life.

She was dozing on the sofa when Dan arrived. Adele answered the door, gave him a glare, and left to listen in from the kitchen. Sitting up, Kim chuckled at her pal's protective instincts.

"Good morning, Detective," she said. "Have a seat. I'm a little sleepy, but I'll help in any way I can."

"Since we're meeting so often, how about we use first names?" Dan asked. "How are you feeling, Kim?"

"Better today, but I'm still tired and achy. Not just my head, but my whole body, from the impact of the crash. Any news?"

"No, the description of the driver of the truck wasn't helpful. He had a ski mask covering his face. That of course, adds to our assumption that the crash was deliberate. Spring in Indiana doesn't require facial covering."

Kim blinked back the tears, feeling hopeless and afraid again. She'd have to stay away from Russ to be safe. It felt like a betrayal of her friend, but he was still in mortal danger, so the people around him were also vulnerable. "I guess you're going to tell me to stay away from Russ, aren't you?"

"I wanted to take a different tack today, if you're up to a few questions," Dan said. "Are you okay?"

He sounded kind and gentle. Surprised at his concern, Kim allowed the tears to flow. "Sure, give me a sec," she said. She massaged her temples and after a minute asked, "What's your new approach?"

"You told me the attacker said something in Russ's place before he hit you," Dan said. "We need to have that information. Can you remember *anything*?"

"It was garbled. The words didn't register, but the emotions sure did. He was cruel, like he enjoyed what he was doing." Kim laid back on the soft pillow, pulling a throw over her to quell the sudden chill she experienced. After a pause, she said, "Maybe something about *deserving* this. Like the attack was punishment or something. I just can't believe Russ has someone around who hates him that much."

"What about you?" Dan looked at Kim and was silent.

"Me? What do you mean? Someone who thought I deserved to be hurt?"

"I'm searching for leads, Kim. Betty Shields told me about your emergency department work. Other than Tom Adams, who is incarcerated, was there anyone else who might hold a grudge because of a psych eval you performed? Or mad about treatment you provided? Maybe an unpleasant custody evaluation where one partner feels wronged?"

"I truly can't think of anyone," Kim answered. "Most of the patients presenting in the ED were suicidal and relieved when I said they should be admitted to a psych unit for their own safety. Their families were also grateful."

"What about patients who could have been seeking drugs?"

"No one stands out," Kim said, pulling the blanket closer. "I didn't just throw patients out onto the streets, you know. After they received appropriate medical care, we provided referrals for housing, food, and counseling. Often the outreach workers would come and pick up the patients and bring them to the shelters or treatment centers for admission if they had nowhere else to go. Again, folks were generally grateful, after they calmed down a bit."

Kim looked out the large living room window onto her pleasant street, wondering about the fallen world she'd landed in so suddenly. "And no, there aren't any other disgruntled clients who come to mind. Most of my ratings from former patients are quite good."

Dan studied Kim's flagging energy. "You're tiring out, aren't you? I'll let you rest. You seem to have had a full morning."

"I was feeling much better, then I learned about the best suspect having a fatal heart attack. That's discouraging."

"Tell him about the rest of your morning," Adele commanded as she entered from the kitchen.

Giving the older woman an icy side-eye, Kim said, "My ex called as well. He'd heard about Russ's situation and wanted to see if I was safe."

"So, you're close to him? What's his name?"

"No, I'm not at all close to Brad Newton. He lives in the Caribbean now. There's nothing between us."

Adele harrumphed again. "Not anymore. Not now that he's got a big bunch of her hard-earned money."

Dan arched his brows. "That sounds interesting. Could he be needing more money from you, Kim?"

"Doubtful," she replied. "The judge made it clear our divorce was settled for good."

Dan looked at Adele, who also arched her brows. "Still, anyone can hire a shady lawyer and reopen a divorce. I'll check Brad Newton out. Kim, you do look really tired. I've taken enough of your time for now."

Adele agreed. "Exactly right, Mr. Westbrook. She's given you all she's got. Maybe you and your partner should start questioning people that Russ and his partner owed money to. I saw on television last night that money is the root of most crimes. The Bible warns us about that, you know."

"Thanks, Mrs. Foley. If I remember my Sunday school lessons correctly though, it's the *love* of money that gets us in trouble. But your point stands. As I said, I'll check into Brad Newton further."

Dan left and Kim felt a little sorry for him. He was doing his best. The lack of progress on the case was annoying him to no end. And he seemed nicer today than in the past, like he might even care about her well-being.

What about his well-being? Did he have a family or a relationship that he could find safe haven in when he was stressed? How did he cope with the pressures of being a detective in a big city? Kim realized she was doing her "psych thing," as Adele put it, but she couldn't help herself. Dan Westbrook seemed like he could use a friend.

_ _ _ _ _ _ _ _ _ _ _ _ _ _

After talking to Kim, Dan made his way back to his office. Kim seemed more worried about Russ Kellams than about herself, which his gut said was a mistake, both on his part and hers. Something was off. Russ Kellams appeared to be a saint, which usually raised his suspicions. But this time he believed the reports of his friends and ex-wife. Kellams was a good man, one who gave back to his community, still had warm feelings for the woman who divorced him, and even paid his firm's debts on his own. Surely Steve Knepper had been responsible for some of the bills, though given the state of his current design firm, he probably didn't have an extra nickel for the cause.

Even Dan knew unadorned brown and beige decor didn't require much professional consultation. *"Sand and mud,"* Alana had called it. He'd have to do some updating to his place if and when he had an extra minute to spare. Maybe he'd add some clouds and sunshine to his sand and mud. Maybe Kim could help him when this was all over. Maybe pigs would fly.

What would a woman like Kim Newton want with him? He was a college-educated detective, but nowhere near the educational level of Dr. Newton. Schooling aside, his life was filled with tracking the worst humans around.

Ugly didn't begin to describe what he dealt with on a daily basis. He still believed that people were basically good, but some days it was a stretch. No, Dr. Newton wouldn't be a suitable partner for a guy who used a gun when the other techniques of persuasion didn't work.

All that aside, Kim had tolerated him on this last visit, even allowing her tears to flow. She'd never been that open with him, and this new development was good for his investigation. It was also good for her perception of him, he admitted to himself. He wanted her to think well of him. He wanted her to know him better, which was nonsense. His focus had to be on the person who had attacked Russ and Kim. Nothing else.

Back at his computer, he did a search on Brad Newton and confirmed what Kim had told him. Newton was in Providenciales, the main resort island of Turks and Caicos. He'd been there for a few years, which his lack of passport activity confirmed. Newton periodically made a little money in hotel wait staff jobs, then took time off until his funds ran low. It was probably a good life, with minimal stress and great weather most of the time. Dan knew Kim's money had funded the small condo Newton had purchased on the beach. He had beachfront property while Kim made do with used furniture and a small bungalow in Broad Ripple. Anger surged in his chest, which surprised him. He felt protective again for Kim, in a way that was separate from the case. Plus, he was imagining a world where she'd help him liven up his apartment. Weird.

Though he knew it would be a dead end, He decided to call Newton. Maybe the freeloader would have some insight into the attacks. Couldn't hurt.

Newton picked up on the second ring. "Hello? Who's this?"

Dan identified himself and offered his badge number should Newton want to verify his identity.

"No need, Detective," Newton said. "I talked to Kim and I know about the attack on Russ."

"What else do you know?" Dan asked. "Do you have any thoughts about the attacks?"

Newton sighed. To Dan's ears, it was forced and executed for dramatic effect. This guy was no grieving ex. Mrs. Foley had him tagged accurately.

"I know you're looking for Russ's enemies," he said. "But you've probably already figured out Russ is a good guy. Sure, he has annoyed colleagues who are envious of his success, but that's part of the creative atmosphere. Those folks are vicious." Newton took a swig of something Dan's gut told him had a good percentage of alcohol. It was early afternoon in Turks and Caicos. Brad Newton liked his booze. Maybe it was part of the island lifestyle. Again, a lifestyle Kim couldn't afford, thanks to Newton.

"As I said, what are your thoughts?" Dan asked again. "Are you implying the focus of the attacks is Kim?"

"She's also a good person," Newton said, after another healthy swallow. "Though she'd say something different about me, I'm sure. But she's got clients who run the gamut in terms of potential for violence. I told her time and time again to focus on the 'worried well' with good insurance, but she wouldn't listen. And the pro bono work got out of hand! She'd spend a good chunk of her time on the people who couldn't pay. If I was a suspicious type, I'd say she did it on purpose when she was supposed to be paying me a portion of her earnings. But that's Kim. She insisted part of her professional duty was to treat those who couldn't afford care. Give me a break."

Dan had a wave of sympathy for Kim. Brad Newton was a self-centered piece of trash. He equated poor people with those who used violence to solve problems. Dan forced himself to consider the information he'd just been given and continued to question Newton.

"Were any of Kim's pro bono clients capable of hurting her?"

"Well, as you're probably aware, she couldn't talk about her cases with me. Professional ethics and all that. But I do know she and the other women in her practice carried pepper spray and made every effort to leave the office together at the end of the evening. They were cautious, and for good reason I would guess."

"But that caution would apply to anyone leaving a place of business after dark, wouldn't it? Surely you had a sense of particular clients Kim was concerned about?"

"Like I said, she wouldn't share that stuff with me," Newton said. "I respected her wishes. We talked about my work, not hers."

Dan suspected Brad hadn't wanted to talk of anything *but* his work, self-absorbed creep that he was. He forced himself to be pleasant. "What did you do for a living in Indianapolis?"

"I was a restaurant manager," Newton replied. "Most of the chains in Indy had the same retail model, so I'd do a good job at one place and then get recruited for more money by another. By the end of our marriage, I knew the menus of every place in town. Kim loves hot wings, and we'd go to the current best place for those." Newton sounded wistful.

Channeling his inner Anson, Dan sympathized. "It's tough to end a marriage, huh? I can relate."

"Yeah, I loved Kim," Newton said softly. "Still do, as a matter of fact. But we weren't good together, and she worked all the time. I got lonely."

Knowing what that really meant, Dan's fury at Newton's infidelity almost surfaced. He forced himself to stay in Anson mode. "Sure, Brad. What's a guy supposed to do when he's alone all the time?"

"I'm not proud of it. Whatever. I'm glad Kim's okay. That's what really matters."

Dan knew Newton was being extra careful to impress him. Anson would have major fun with this guy. Dan, not so much. He made another effort not to get irritated. "Sure, I get it. But back to who could have hurt Kim. If you had to guess, was there anyone who stood out? Like when Kim came home, did she slip and tell you anything about somebody who scared her?"

Newton paused. After another loud gulp of his beverage, he said, "Well that one ED case was public knowledge. It happened after I moved down here, so I wasn't around for all of that ugliness. He really worked her over financially. And since he's in prison now, he'd be off your list. And to repeat, Kim didn't share confidential stuff with me."

She shared plenty with you, Dan thought. Lots of her money, for example. Her love and loyalty while you were cheating on her. He forced himself to be professional and thanked Newton for his help. The man in the beach condo was effusive in his fake offer to help anytime. Poor Kim. He hoped they hadn't been married long. She deserved so much better.

He decided to rerun all his previous leads. He exhausted his sources, reread all the interview transcripts, and was about to grab lunch when he remembered Tom Adams. He was incarcerated, but why not check again? Maybe something from the trial would lead to an accomplice who had a grudge against Kim.

A few mouse clicks later, he blinked at the computer screen. This couldn't be possible. Adams had been released to a senior rehab facility two weeks ago. His charm had not served him well in prison, since the reason for his new housing was a severe beating by fellow inmates causing kidney damage. He required temporary dialysis, and because he'd been cited for good behavior, was allowed to live in the assisted living facility wearing an ankle bracelet while his kidneys healed. Dan knew instantly who Kim's attacker was. Russ Kellams had been a diversion, useful to Adams as a way to get to Kim.

"Are you kidding me?" he shouted to the empty cubicle.

Anson walked over, puzzled. "What did you find? Anything helpful?"

Dan filled him in, full of frustration that they'd been spinning their wheels and ignoring Tom Adams.

"Yeah, the IT guy was in a few days ago and mentioned some kind of glitch. He said it was almost fixed." He studied Dan's angry, stricken face. "What's our next move, Dan?"

CHAPTER SEVEN

"I'M GOING TO START with the place Adams has been living," Dan mumbled. "They'd better have been watching him around the clock."

He called the facility, Northside Plaza, and asked for the administrator. Mr. Mathew McKinter was jovial, cooperative, and totally clueless about Adams's danger to other residents and those outside the complex. Dan wasn't sure if such cluelessness was a result of not knowing Adams's history or of being happy to fill an empty bed paid for in full by the penal system.

According to McKinter, Adams was a model resident. "I tell you, Detective, Tom is basically a fine man," McKinter protested. "I think he's one of those guys who made some poor choices and is paying for his lack of judgment." McKinter answered a question from someone in the background and continued. "I've got to go in a minute. Morning staff huddles wait for no one," he said, full of self-importance. Obviously, his superior administrative skills were necessary in such meetings. Dan was sure that McKinter had never worked at a bedside or provided actual care to vulnerable patients.

"Anyway, Tom's a hit with all our female residents, as you might guess. There's a shortage of older fellas in a place like ours, so a young stud like Tom is a welcome addition. I'm just sorry he's going to be released back to prison in a few weeks. My residents have been in a much better mood since he's been here. Fortunately for him, and unfortunately for us, his kidneys are healing well."

Dan wanted to reach through the line, or cloud, or whatever transmitted phone messages, and strangle McKinter. What an idiot. He calmed himself and asked, "What sort of security watch has Adams been under while he's been in your care?"

"The usual," McKinter answered. "Since we're not located in Indianapolis proper, our county jail sends whoever is free to stand watch. But given the safety provided by Tom's ankle bracelet, there were a few days he was unattended. I looked in on him periodically those days. Nothing seemed out of the ordinary. When he wasn't at dialysis, he attended Bingo, did crafts, and as I said, flirted with all the ladies."

Dan's slow boil continued to simmer. "Mr. McKinter, where did you do your criminology training?"

"What?" he sputtered. "I have a degree in healthcare management, Mr. Westbrook."

"Exactly," Dan said, this information verifying McKinter's lack of real expertise in the provision of health care. "Your idea of 'looking in' on Tom Adams is comparable

to petting an alligator. Stupid and asking for a big bite."
Dan took a deep breath, forced himself to stay polite and
continued. "What about his visits to the dialysis center?
Did his driver stay the whole time?"

Catching on, suddenly McKinter was cold and calculating. "Detective, I assure you Mr. Adams has been
provided the care the prison system contracted for. Our
services are second to none. Be aware that our rating is
one of the highest in the Indianapolis metro area, which
includes all the surrounding counties, by the way. Obviously, our drivers have to tend to other residents' needs
during appointments. When a medical appointment is
completed, the resident calls our driver and arranges to be
picked up. Tom was very faithful in calling the minute his
dialysis was finished."

Odd, Dan thought. This guy went from being a good
old boy to a man spouting lawsuit avoidance phrases.
What did that mean? Well, it probably meant Adams
had been free to do whatever he wanted when he was
out of the facility. "Mr. McKinter, I think we're done
for now. By five o'clock this afternoon, I want you to
fax me a detailed schedule of Tom Adams's whereabouts
since the day of his admission to your facility. Be sure
to include an hour-by-hour accounting of his activities.
I need to know when he ate, participated in your activities, had physical therapy, and was transported to and
from dialysis. Most importantly, I will be checking on
times when Adams was not guarded or observed by others. Understood?"

McKinter huffed into the phone line. "I understand, Detective. I'll do my best."

"Do better than your best," Dan said. As he ended the call, he knew McKinter would delegate the task to an underling. He doubted the record of Adams's daily schedule would be accurate. His gut told him records were fudged frequently at Northside when lawsuits threatened. And in this case, there was a powerful incentive to say that Adams was observed all the time.

Anson walked by his desk as Dan muttered a satisfying swear word. "What's up, Dan?"

"Lots, unfortunately. I've got a solid lead on who attacked Russ Kellams. As I suspected, our perp didn't really target Russ. He was after Kim. We've been wasting our time this whole week."

He filled Anson in on the release of Adams from prison for dialysis and about Kim's memory of the attacker saying someone "deserved" it. "The administrator at the senior living facility has been treating Adams like a hero, not a felon. Adams has had a free run of the place, and who knows how often he's been out and about."

"What about the ankle bracelet?" Anson asked. "Wouldn't those records show Adams wasn't where he was supposed to be?"

"They should, but you know those things can be hacked or tampered with," Dan said. "Adams is a psychopath. He'd figure it out or have friends who could."

"What now?" Anson was angry, too. "We need to warn Dr. Newton."

"I'll do it," Dan said. "This isn't an update to deliver over the phone." He pulled on his jacket and added, "I've been missing Kim's buddy, Adele."

Anson laughed. "Yeah, I think Mrs. Foley likes you." He studied Dan for a few seconds. "I also think you like the good doctor. Watch yourself, Dan."

Thirty minutes later, Dan pulled in front of Kim's house. He saw the curtains on the front window part and knew Adele would meet him at the door. When she did, he was ready.

"Good afternoon, Mrs. Foley," he said. "I'm sorry to return so soon, but I'm happy to see you again. I'm glad you're staying with Kim. She needs you more than you know."

Mollified before she could give him grief, Adele nodded and waved him in.

"Has something happened, Detective? Is Kim in danger?"

"Why would I be in danger?" a soft voice asked. Kim had the muddled look of a person just up from a hard nap. "Adele, what's Dan talking about?"

"Kim, there's been a development. Let's all sit down and talk it through. Mrs. Foley, could you get Kim a drink? A soda or water?"

"I'll be right back with tea for all of us," Adele said.

Kim drew a breath. Instead of filling with tears, her eyes glinted with anger, as if she sensed what was coming. "What's going on, Dan?"

Adele entered and distributed the supposedly soothing herbal tea. Dan choked down a sip and began. "I rechecked

Tom Adams's whereabouts. Unfortunately, he's been released with an ankle bracelet because he needs temporary outpatient dialysis. Between dialysis sessions, he's been living the good life in a senior living facility." He studied Kim's worried face, hating what he was about to tell her.

"He can't be out of prison! But even if he is, the monitoring device will keep track of him, right? And why would he attack Russ?"

"Those devices can be tampered with. Knowing our friend Adams, he got someone to fiddle with it so he can come and go more than it shows." Dan wanted to sit by Kim, to comfort her. Sadly, Adele had beaten him to the prime position on the sofa.

"Russ was in all likelihood a decoy. Adams was probably following you for about a week before the attack. He knew precisely when you'd be walking Russ's dog. Now we have to prove that he was the attacker. We should have asked you this before, but did you have any physical contact with him? Did you lash out or scratch him?"

Kim's breathing was coming fast and shallow. Adele gently pushed Kim's head between her legs and rubbed her back. As before, Dan wanted to be the one next to Kim, helping her deal with the repugnant horror she was reliving. He'd have to revisit the meaning of that desire later.

A minute later, Kim sat up, her color better and breathing regular. "No, I was on the floor before I knew what was happening. First I was trying to soothe Reed and then I was talking to the EMT."

So, no hope for DNA evidence. "That's okay, Kim. We'll figure this out and Adams will be back where he belongs soon. In the meantime, is there any place you can go? Somewhere out of town where Adams can't find you?"

"Sam and I had a condo on Lake Michigan. It's been locked up for a season, but it's livable," Adele offered. "We could go there."

"That's a great thought, Mrs. Foley. You and Kim should pack and hit the road this evening. The sooner you're gone, the better."

Kim stood. Her breathing was still steady as she strode to Dan's chair. "I'm not running, Dan. That pig won't get me a second time. I'll be ready."

To Dan's surprise, Adele defended his suggestion. "Now honey, don't be foolish. There's no shame in staying safe. Those self-defense lessons won't help against a devil like Tom Adams." She paused and Dan was shocked to see her burst into tears. "Kimmy, Candi and I took care of you the first time Adams attacked you. None of us can get through that again."

Kim returned to the seat by Adele. Hugging her friend, she said, "I can, and I will deal with him. I'm done living in fear. That's the reason I've started sleeping well. I'm strong enough. Trust me."

Adele looked at Dan. He couldn't believe she was now his ally. Not that it was helping much. Kim was a stubborn and foolish woman if she thought she could take Tom Adams on.

"Listen, Kim. Think like Adams for a second. The first time he attacked you, he stole your identity. He was enraged you'd barred his admission to the hospital. But that wasn't enough for him. He beat you and nearly raped you. Now you've caused his prison sentence. That's a big difference from the slap on the hand most identity thieves get. My gut says now he's out to kill you. And before he does that, you'll suffer. He'll make sure of it."

Adele nodded and put her arm around Kim's shoulders. "He's right, Kim. Men like Adams lust after revenge. They like the hunt and relish the takedown."

It was Dan's turn to nod. Oddly enough, the television shows Adele was watching were serving him well. If only Kim would buy in. A safe house in Michigan, even with an elderly partner, was better than staying in Indianapolis.

"Adele, you're correct," Kim said. "Tom will enjoy the hunt, whether I'm in Michigan or Indianapolis. He'd probably be in your condo before we were. I imagine he'd fake another injury, or even hurt himself to stay out of prison while he looked for me. What kind of protection can you offer me here, Dan?"

"Minimal, I'm afraid," he responded. "Our force is short of manpower, womanpower, even canines." He paused and began to think out loud. "I could stay with you, I suppose. We've done it before, when witnesses were about to testify. This is still an active case, so I'll have to get it cleared by the powers that be." He knew it would be a hard sell, but since the case had gotten so much press due to Russ's public persona, he hoped he'd prevail with administration.

Kim nodded. "I'd be glad to make the case with your superiors," she said. "Understandably, Tom Adams has been a psychological study of mine since he attacked me. Let me write something up before you talk to your boss."

"Good idea. In the meantime, I want you to stay put, and Mrs. Foley needs to be here constantly. No running out to do a quick errand, no grocery delivery, no walks around the block to get fresh air. Kim, you're going to be a prisoner in your own home for a while."

Both women bobbed their heads in agreement. "Understood, Dan," Kim said. "But that means you'll have to be our delivery person in addition to our guard. Is that okay?"

"It's okay if it works. We'll *make* it work. Let me get back to you about the specifics. I hope to talk to you by this evening. What can I bring before I move in?"

- - - - - - - - - - - - - -

Surprisingly, Dan's boss had already talked to the chief of police about protection for Russ and Kim. Anson's intervention detailing the computer snafu had helped, for which Dan was grateful. Since Kim was now the sole person requiring a guard, Dan received permission to fill that role within hours. He walked up Kim's porch steps that evening at eight o'clock.

Adele Foley greeted him with a side hug and a finger to her lips. "Hush now, Detective. Kim's sleeping for the night. She worked for several hours after you left, writing up a psych profile on that scumbag Adams. Do you need it to convince your superiors that you should stay here?"

Shocked by Adele's sweet greeting and use of television slang, Dan shook his head and smiled. "No need, Mrs. Foley. But I'd like to read it, if you don't think Kim would mind. It might give us clues she's not even aware of."

Patting his back, Adele led him to Kim's recliner and handed him a sheaf of papers. "What can I bring you, Detective? Have you eaten?"

"Thanks, Mrs. Foley. Please call me Dan. And yes, I've eaten, but coffee would be nice."

"Coming right up. And you can call me Adele," she said. Blushing a little, she fled to the kitchen.

Dan marveled at the loyalty Kim seemed to generate. The hospital staff, her friends and neighbors, Russ Kellams, everyone who knew her was anxious she receive only the best care and protection. He vowed he'd be the one to keep her safe and catch Adams. He sipped the coffee Adele delivered and began to digest the psych report Kim had exhausted herself preparing for him. He hoped she was as good a psychologist as she was beautiful.

His wish was granted. It was unlike any psychological profile he'd ever read. Most of the reports were detailed with full historical accounts of the perpetrator's life. True to form, the prison report he'd read on Tom Adams covered his coddled childhood upbringing, his brilliant academic performance in college, and his surprising inability to hold a job. Narcissistic personality disorder was the primary diagnosis, totally omitting Adams's psychopathic behaviors.

Kim's report had much more depth. Even during his college years, Adams had been accused three times of date rape. Kim's ED history had revealed this; Dan was sure Adams had been bragging about his prowess indirectly. Dan was astounded to read Adams had never had any serious repercussions from the accusations. The conclusions were always couched in the vague "he said, she said" verbiage. In each case the woman who had accused Adams transferred out of the university rather than exist where he roamed free.

Kim had contacted the college where Adams had been a student over ten years ago. While no one would talk to her due to confidentiality concerns, she'd been able to dig up a Twitter account authored by one of the women who had accused Adams of rape. Adams had ridiculed the woman's unusual first name when Kim did the ED history, so she was relatively easy to find. Per Kim's report, after the attack the author had been encouraged by the college administration to either transfer or finish her degree online. Adams's incarceration had caused the woman's feed to explode with new followers, some of whom spoke of similar interactions with Adams, even after he left the college.

So, his ability to abuse women continues, Dan thought. Adams's presence in a facility of vulnerable older women made his skin crawl. And what about the staff? Most employees in such places were female, making little money, and probably susceptible to a good-looking man.

No wonder he's so entitled. He does what he wants, even after being in prison. He could have arranged his own beating, just to get close to Kim. The assault on him had been more violent than Adams would have planned, and that made Dan smile. Hoping Adams had suffered immense pain, he turned back to the pages Kim had written.

Rather than focusing on Tom's past, Kim had highlighted current behaviors. She wrote about the emergency department visit, during which Adams begged for pain relief and a hospital bed for the night. He had even faked tremors, which Kim and the ED staff knew were bogus. Small wonder he was enraged at her refusal to hospitalize him.

Then the report turned to Kim's "pure professional speculation," as she labeled the next section. Speaking of Adams as she would a character in a novel, Kim wrote of his narcissism, his need to dominate and win, and his violent mood swings. She generated vignettes during which Tom Adams tried to con people, including his attempt to be hospitalized, which Kim attributed to a need to perfect his grifting skills. Kim also highlighted his probable reaction when his efforts were thwarted. In each case, he became violent. As his frustration grew, so did his violence.

Kim obviously knew what Adams was capable of. Her refusal to go into hiding was a puzzle. Why wouldn't she seek safety? Her last vignette answered his question.

Tom Adams would always be able to track his prey with the help of at least one person in charge of his care. *She's right, he'd be in Michigan before she was. And someone was helping him. He had to find out who that was.*

Dan called Anson early the next day. He gave his partner the latest background on Adams. After procuring Adams's dialysis schedule from McKinter at Northside and ensuring Adams was "off" today, Anson agreed to use his many charms to interview the staff at the dialysis center and get back to Dan asap.

CHAPTER EIGHT

"HI, IS THIS THE right place?" Anson asked. "I have an appointment with Angela Hess, but I'm a little early."

An attractive, deeply tanned woman of about forty smiled at him. "I'm Angie Hess. You're Anson, correct? My notes say you're looking for a dialysis center for your grandfather."

"Exactly," Anson said with his killer smile. "My grandpa's current place is not a good fit, to put it mildly. He gets so depressed after his treatments, which I know is partly normal, but he's always complaining that he's surrounded by old folks waiting to die."

Angie nodded sympathetically in response. "I understand. Kidney disease is primarily confined to the elderly, and it's hard on them. For what it's worth, we have a fair number of younger folks on our caseload. That might help your grandfather's mood. They're a chatty bunch."

Feigning interest in Angie's caseload, Anson perked up. "Really? Could you tell me a little about the younger patients?" Noting Angie's hesitation, he added, "Without revealing anything confidential, of course."

"I guess that would be okay," the nurse said. "Well, we have one temporary patient who's real popular with the staff and patients. He listens to everyone's story, which is fairly rare. Usually, patients want to talk about their illness trajectory, how they ended up in the 'chair' and what they're afraid of going forward."

"Temporary? I thought dialysis was pretty much a life sentence."

Angie nodded. "Sometimes patients get dialysis in the hospital for a short time, or like this fellow, had injuries that required outpatient dialysis while his kidneys healed." She hesitated, and then said, "Poor guy. He was severely beaten. He's lucky he's recovering kidney function."

"What a tough break," Anson said, full of sympathy. "The streets are full of danger. Hope his mugging wasn't too bad."

The head nurse looked haunted and shook her head. "He'll be fine. Actually, he takes walks after his sessions. He says it helps him ground himself."

Anson noted her blush and pushed further. "He sounds like a good guy. I'm glad he'll get better." He winked at the nurse. "I sense you like him. It's hard not to get involved with patients you see so frequently, huh?"

The blush reddened further. "Yeah, he's a special man." She recovered and said, "Let me tell you about some of the other patients, then I'll give you a tour of the facility."

Anson agreed and was given the tour and a tedious summary of the patient caseload, topped off with a cup of bitter coffee in the staff break room. During that time, he discovered what he'd hoped for and more.

- - - - - - - - - - - - - -

Anson was admitted to Kim's house by Adele, who had her fingers to her lips. Kim was sleeping in again, which everyone hoped was a good thing.

"Bingo! Jackpot! Ka-Ching!" Anson whispered.

Dan eyed his partner. The charmer had obviously come through. "Tell me everything."

"It took a minute, but Nurse Angie eventually opened up about her favorite patient, Tom."

"She said his name?" Dan asked.

"Yep. I got the impression since Adams is about to be discharged, she was on the hunt for another guy. I fit the bill." Anson chugged his coffee and added more sugar. "Do you want to hear the best part?"

Dan nodded, afraid he was hoping for too much.

"Turns out Adams has convinced Angie he needs a walk after each treatment. The walks are getting longer and longer. When Angie first expressed her concern, he followed her into the supply closet and they 'got friend-ly.' She admitted what a great kisser he was, and that they were in there for almost thirty minutes. Later, he apologized later for his 'bold behavior.' Angie said she felt used, but then she said how lonely she was. To use her jargon, 'he caught her at a vulnerable moment.' I couldn't decide if I felt sorry for her or disgusted at her weakness."

Dan couldn't believe what he was hearing. "Come on. It can't have been that easy for Adams to seduce the head of the center."

"I got the whole story. On Adams's first day, an older guy coded midway into his session. The center was understaffed, so the whole skeleton crew worked on the patient while they waited for the EMTs. Angie agreed to let Tom take a walk since it was 'so distressing' for him to see the old guy getting CPR. She didn't admit he was a felon out for medical treatment."

"I'll bet he was distressed," Dan said. "So distressed he got to walk all around Indy. Who knows what he's been able to do? He probably hired a ride share to get to Kellams's place so his 'walk' wouldn't last too long."

"It gets better. She finally told me Tom was a prisoner currently housed at an assisted living center. Angie's convinced he was wrongfully convicted. He's so slick he told her it was a blessing the old guy died after he coded. He gave her some baloney about health care resources being overused by the elderly. When she saw my shock, she emphasized my grandfather would receive the best care available."

Dan rubbed his temples. What gall. What sick manipulations. He, Kim, and Russ were up against a truly evil foe. They had to catch him, and soon.

"Okay, the 'walks' are enough to arrest Adams for violating his terms of release. But I think we should wait. He'll bust those charges easily."

"I've got more," Anson said. He looked disgusted, even more than a minute ago.

"What? What more could there be?"

"Angie said Tom told her about a woman who'd broken his heart. They had that in common, since Angie had a recent breakup also." Anson rolled his eyes. "Anyway, Adams told Angie he'd seen his 'ex' on one of his walks, and it broke his heart all over again. He said his old girlfriend had been abusive in the past, kicking him and scratching his face, so he was careful she didn't see him. But since he still loves her, he needed to be close to a 'real woman' to heal."

Barely able to listen, Dan forced himself to ask, "What else did he say about his supposed ex?"

Anson hesitated. "She said the ex-girlfriend was into humiliating 'poor Tom.' She enjoyed pointing out his weaknesses and mistakes, especially in front of others. He even told Angie the former girl had landed him in jail on trumped up abuse charges."

Dan connected the dots. "How rough has he been with Angie Hess?"

"There's the million-dollar question. I asked her directly and she hedged. She admitted their supply closets trysts have become a little tough at times. Adams has pushed her against the wall and took some convincing to stop when she told him they were going too far. Luckily, a patient wanting a snack before his treatment saved her by pounding on the closet door."

Dan swallowed as the bile threatened to enter his throat. "Great work, Anson. The important question is if Hess was on to you. Did she make you as a cop?"

"No way," Anson answered. "I asked all the right kidney questions, to put it crudely. And I'd read up on special diets for dialysis. She was impressed by my knowledge. I also shared that my grandfather cheated on his diet all the time. Angie laughed and said that was the norm."

"Still, are you sure she didn't think you were IMPD?"

"No, I repeated I was there for my grandfather and how close we were. I told her I appreciated her honesty, and that I've been through my share of breakups, and that my mind had been messed with, too. She agreed to call me in a few weeks about new openings for my grandfather."

"That will be too late," Dan said. "We've got to figure out how to nail this creep."

"Yep," Adele agreed.

Anson left for the office, carrying a sack full of food from Adele.

- - - - - - - - - - - - -

Kim woke to the enticing scent of fresh coffee. She heard the sizzle of bacon on the griddle and chug of the toaster as it popped up. Brunch, a la Adele Foley, was almost ready. The woman didn't believe in a granola bar eaten on the run while commuting to work. No, breaking the fast was the most important meal of the day, to be relished and savored.

"Good morning, Kim," Dan said as she entered the eat-in kitchen. He sipped his juice and seemed to study her. "How was your night?"

Annoyed but at the same time grateful he was in her house, she smiled. "It was fine. No nightmares or sudden awakenings. I must have sensed your presence."

"I'm glad you were able to rest. You compiled quite a study of Adams. It couldn't have helped your quest for a good night's sleep."

"Oddly, it did help me," she admitted as she drank her own cup of Adele's strong brew. "I was reminded of his severe pathology. All that drivel about his understandable narcissism in the prison report is so incomplete. Narcissists aren't all violent. But Adams is."

"I'm happy to hear that assessment," Dan said, the relief clear in his eyes. "Adams is the worst kind of offender in many ways. He's handsome, charming, self-aware, and smart. He's intelligent enough to slip in acts of kindness just often enough to throw his marks off. He probably helps little old ladies cross the street and puts away their groceries every once in a while." Dan thought a second. "Actually, he *has* been helping little old ladies while he's been at Northside."

"Creep," Adele interjected.

"Tell me something, Dan," Kim asked between bites of her breakfast. "Why don't you like psychologists? You sound surprised that I consider Adams a true threat. Why is that?"

Dan spun his fork around on the table. "Time for full disclosure, I guess. My ex-wife and I did some couples counseling before our divorce. All the blame landed on me. Seemed unfair, though I'll admit I wasn't around much, what with my job and all."

"I'm sorry that was the impression the counselor gave you," Kim said. "Marital therapy is tough, definitely not my favorite thing to do. And it's been my experience that marriages don't fail due to only one member of the couple. There's usually a tangled mess of history, unspoken expectations, and mistakes on both parts." Kim was lost in thought for a minute. "And before you ask, I'd include my marriage in that statement. I could have done a few things differently with Brad."

"What do you mean?" Dan's brows lifted.

"Oh, I'd have been more aware of how lonely Brad was. I did work terrible hours because I was trying to pay off my student loans from grad school. He spent a lot of time alone, especially in the evenings. Then our weekends were devoted to catching up from our work weeks. He worked a lot of hours, too, so we'd split chores to keep the house looking decent. And there were groceries to buy, bills to pay, all that." Kim eyes lowered.

Making a pass through the living room, Adele weighed in. "That's baloney, Kim. Brad was a big baby who needed constant pampering. I refuse to let you assume blame for the end of your marriage to that conniving man."

"Thanks, Adele, but you're wrong. First, I'm not assuming *all* the blame. I'm just owning my share. In addition to my long hours, I needed a lot of quiet time when I got home.

Therapy drained me when I was starting out. Often Brad and I wouldn't talk beyond pleasantries until the morning, when we were both in a rush to start the day all over again."

"I stand by my baloney comment," Adele said.

Dan and Kim burst into laughter together. Kim wondered what it would be like to have Dan around to laugh with. Would he have resented her long hours and her need for quiet times after coming home? She knew in her bones Dan wouldn't have been as needy as Brad. If Dan felt neglected, he would be certain to bring it up and they would work together to solve the issue. None of which Brad did or was even capable of doing.

"Wish I'd had you as a therapist," Dan muttered. "Of course, my ex was happy with our guy's work. And I paid the entire bill."

Kim winced. "Again, I'm sorry, Dan. I hope the experience wasn't a total waste. Did you find anything useful about it?"

"I'll admit I worked too much, like you, which then made me distant from my wife. Anson had been telling me that all along. And his input was free." Dan chuckled, lightening the mood.

"I resent what you said earlier," Adele called out from the kitchen as she loaded the dishwasher. "Little old ladies like me aren't dumb. We can spot a phony a mile away."

Kim grinned, enjoying Dan's embarrassment. "I'm sure it was just an example," she said to Adele. "Right, Dan?"

"Right. I'm sorry Adele. I'm ageist to the core. It bothers me to admit it, since I'm not getting any younger. My point was Tom Adams is shrewd enough to play at being a Boy Scout when needed. I'll bet some of the prison staff have sympathy for his being beaten."

A muffled, "You betcha!" was Adele's response from the kitchen.

"What's our next step?" Kim asked. "Do you want to go over my schedule for the next few weeks?"

"I thought you were taking time off," Dan said. His face reddened. "You need to stay home, Kim. You're not safe anywhere outside the front porch."

"I know, I know. My appointments for the next month are all telehealth. I've got my dog duties covered, too. Good thing I hired that college kid to help out during May."

"Which was my idea, if I recall," Adele interjected. "Good thing, indeed."

"What's the month of May got to do with needing extra help?" Dan asked.

"It's Indy 500 month," Kim said. "I always help Russ with his showplace motorhome. He parks it on the racetrack grounds to display his latest designs. The powers that be are in full approval, since most of the drivers have big RVs and are always in the market to replace them." She smiled at the memories flooding over her.

"He's done it for so many years that his local clients make it part of the race week experience. They love to look at Russ's design and hope to spot a driver in between their practice sessions. I'm there during the times he's covering his office or running errands."

Still confused, Dan asked again. "Still don't get it. Now you're a design team member? Of a double wide?"

"*Not* a double wide," Kim said. "Well, I'm a designer of sorts. Russ has taught me so much, and I took a few design courses in grad school to help alleviate the stress of clinical work. Basically, I show folks his design boards, how he's incorporated his ideas into the motorhome, talk about what could be possible in their own houses or RVs, and hand out his cards. He's so creative that the place looks different each year. And it's fun meeting new people."

Kim ate several more bites of her bacon sandwich in between gulps of orange juice. She was famished but energized at the same time. "This year is even more crucial. Instead of renting, Russ has actually purchased the motor home, to the tune of over a million dollars. He hopes to sell it at a big profit to refill his bank account. Paying off all the debts from K&K Interiors nearly did him in. Dan, I need to be there. It's just open to the public for the weekend of the race."

Undeterred by Dan's glare, Kim launched her sales pitch. "Let me explain, Dan. It's not the standard RV that you're used to. Russ purposely picked a million-plus dollar vehicle this year. And that's wholesale and stripped down, with no luxury appliances, no custom fittings, just a high-end motor, with little in the way of pleasing décor."

Dan eyes were wide. "All I heard was a million plus. He had the money to purchase it? You're kidding, right?

How fancy does it need to be? Hooking up at a campground and making a fire doesn't require pleasing *décor*."

Kim sighed. She had her work cut out for her with this man. "Most of the buyers of high-end RVs aren't camping in the traditional sense. Actually, if you tour the grounds at the Speedway track, you'll see the drivers often own one or more of these rides," she repeated. "There's a whole parking lot close to the garages for the motorhomes owned by the race teams. It becomes a little city of its own during May. Who wants to stay in a hotel for the majority of the season when you can sleep on a mattress that you've chosen, hang out with your colleagues, and walk back to your home?"

"But why call it camping? In my mind, a pup tent, constant bug bites, and dirty, sweaty clothes make for real camping. These guys are way too coddled."

"Okay, so it's not camping in the Indiana sense. Plus, 'these guys' aren't coddled in the way you think. They put their lives on the line for their profession. These homes serve a real purpose. Drivers need to eat and sleep well so they're on the top of their game. They have personal chefs, fitness regimens, and sports psychologists. They need a space of their own to meet their complex training needs. When Russ is finished with the vehicles, they're worth way more than the purchase price."

"More than a million? How can that be?"

"Italian leather couches, massage chairs, multiple baths, two heat pump units, generators with back-up solar panels. Want me to start on the kitchen?"

"Why not?" Dan leaned back, clearly humoring her.

Kim didn't care about Dan's dismissive stance. She had to make him understand that the RV was crucial to Russ's career, so she began to tick off the features of the cooking area. "Premier appliances, marble countertops. Induction cooktop and convection oven with an air fryer. Also, the home has four televisions and a state-of-the-art sound system. Or maybe you'd be more impressed by the mechanics. Comfortable suspension, mega horsepower engine, and four slide-outs. Honestly, Dan, it's a palace on wheels."

"I don't care if it's *Buckingham Palace*, you can't be there this year, Kim. That would be an ideal place for Adams to get to you." Taking note of Kim's pursed lips, he added, "Not up for discussion."

Kim was turning pink. "You're being a bully, Dan."

"No, I'm being a cop. A small, enclosed space makes you totally vulnerable. Adams could hide and wait until everyone has left. He'll disable Russ, or worse, and then start on you. It won't be pretty, Kim."

"We'll see," Kim said. She turned away but saw Adele roll her eyes. "Not you, too! Adele, you can't agree with Dan, can you?"

"Finish your bacon sandwich," Adele ordered as she wiped the counters. "Of course I agree with Dan. You're asking for trouble if you think you'll be safe. Think of it. The roar of the car noise and the music from Carb Day, then Legends Day, and then the race would disguise any screams for help you might be able to generate. Think, Kim. Think."

Kim was thinking, all right. Tom Adams had her imprisoned in her own home. This could go on forever. Even if his dialysis ended and he was sent back to prison, the possibility of his parole would always be a threat. His mind would be hatching new plans by the hour. And he would parlay more good behavior to decrease his sentence. He could even engineer another beating to get him out for more medical treatment. She would never be safe unless this ended soon. She refused to look over her shoulder for the rest of her life.

More to the point, she was tired of being a victim. Once again, all the pithy phrases she'd said to patients came back to convict her. What about God's never-ending protection? What about God's assurance that the righteous would prevail? Praying for God to give her wisdom, she faced Dan and Adele. God's lightbulb came on, and she decided to switch tactics.

"Listen, both of you. I appreciate your advice and concern. Adams is smart, and he would love the chance to trap me in the motorhome. So, let's give it to him! Surely between the three of us we can figure out a plan to trap *him*. Dan, your partner could help too, right?" Noting the skeptical looks leveled in her direction, she used her diversionary topic. "Anyway, it's days before the RV open house. I have to go to Terre Haute this afternoon. Adele can drive since I'm not safe behind the wheel."

Adele hooted. "What? You're going to take a road trip when that evil monster is on the loose?"

"Don't you remember? I promised Mom I'd lay flowers on her sister's grave for the Memorial Day holiday." Kim looked at Dan and winced at his look of disapproval.

"My aunt was a Viet Nam veteran," Kim explained. "She was a nurse and qualifies as a real hero. Unfortunately, she also developed a substance use problem. She died a few years ago from the ravages of alcohol addiction. Mom still feels guilty that she couldn't help her."

"You're not going anywhere without me," Dan said. "Adele, you're off the hook."

CHAPTER NINE

DAN COULDN'T BELIEVE HIS ears. The drive to Terre Haute was the least of his problems with Kim. This intelligent, savvy woman wanted to be bait for a violent criminal in a noisy, chaotic, uncontrollable environment. Not that he had any other ideas. The crucial thing was to catch Adams in the act of attempting to harm Kim. They could nail him violating the parameters of his being off the Northside campus and away from the dialysis center, but he'd beat those charges quickly. They needed to witness his cruelty toward Kim. Dan shuddered at the thought.

He decided to play for time. "Back to your question, Kim. Sure, Anson could help, if the upper-level folks agree." He had a bite of crunchy bacon, enjoying its unique flavor. "Adele, what did you do to this bacon? It's a little sweet."

Grinning, Adele responded. "I dust it a little with brown sugar, Dan. I make sure it's not on the griddle too long when it's been sugared so it doesn't burn. Tasty, huh?"

"It's wonderful," he mumbled between bites. Kim glared at him, savvy to his distracting tactics. "But back to the plan. We need one. Kim as a sitting duck is no plan. Let's give this some thought and reconvene tomorrow morning."

"Agreed," Kim said. "But it's going to happen, Dan. I refuse to be one of Adams's permanent victims. By Memorial Day, this saga will be over."

Adele and Dan stared. He couldn't help himself when he said, "Over as in you being safe. Not dead."

Ignoring his dire warning, Kim continued with her line of thinking. "I'm trying to figure out where you'll hide, Dan. The motorhome is one of the largest models made, but still tiny in terms of keeping your big frame hidden."

"The bathroom is the obvious place," Adele said. "But I have a feeling Adams will case the place before he tries to hurt you. He'd look there first thing."

"True," Kim said. "There's an upper storage cubby over the bed in the main sleeping area." Studying Dan, she tilted her head. "How tall are you?"

"Six-one," he answered. "Too tall to be folded into any kind of storage area. Surely you see this is impossible, Kim. You'll be all alone. Even if Anson and I are hidden outside or under the motorhome, Adams could assault or even kill you before we got in. You're going to have to tell Russ to get a different helper this year."

"Nope, this is the perfect setup," Kim said. "Adams will be seduced by the opportunity to have me to himself in a secluded spot. He'll make sure no one is around. Maybe I could even schedule a fake date with him before or after show house hours. He'll even lock the door from the inside once the home is empty of visitors. It's perfect!"

Adele and Dan looked at each other. Adele spoke first. "Kimmy, is your head hurting? Are you dizzy? You're not thinking right. You've got yourself locked up with Adams and smiling at the prospect."

Dan was more to the point. "It's ridiculous, Kim." With a sudden look of awareness, he added, "You plan to be armed, don't you?"

"Sure do," she answered. "I've got Adele's gun and the knowledge to use it properly. I'd never entertain the notion of being alone with Adams without something to defend myself with."

Dan repeated himself. "It's ridiculous, Kim. Sure, you're probably a good shot at the range, but in close quarters with a psychopath intent on assaulting you prior to your death, it's different. He'd have the gun before you knew what was happening."

"Then that's a possibility we need to noodle on," Kim said, oblivious to his concern. "As I said before, we need a plan." She looked away and considered Dan's scary scenario. "Yes, I could be disarmed easily, couldn't I? One punch from Adams and I'd be off balance or on the floor, giving him enough time to get the gun."

Adele weighed in. "Remember, Kim, he's punched you before. Slapped you, tried to strip you. He's stronger than you, no doubt about it. You want to show us you've healed, and you have, but you can't get around his physical superiority."

"There is no plan for such a risky idea," Dan grumbled. "You can't be alone. I need to be in there with you. That's what we have to figure out."

"Could you be in disguise?" Adele asked.

Kim laughed and pointed to Dan. "This guy looks like a cop through and through. He's tall, fit, and suspicious of everyone. It would be like putting the Big Bad Wolf in sheep's clothing." Her eyes widened and she smiled at the thought and seemed to be wondering about Dan's softer side.

Dan sensed Kim was "noodling" about more than just the plan to trap Adams. "What's the smile about?" he said with a grin. He knew she was thinking about him. Her dreamy look practically invited him to kiss her. If Adele wasn't around, he'd have done it.

"Nothing. You can't be disguised, which means we've got to figure out where to hide you." She lowered her gaze, mentally going over the floor plan of Russ's RV.

"Still noodling?" Dan asked. "This plan of yours will never work, you know. There's no way we'll sign off on it."

Kim ignored him. "There's a large L-shaped sectional sofa in the living area. It's a fold-out bed with side storage for the linens. What would you think about asking Russ to have the bed removed from inside the sofa?"

Dan blanched. "You can't be serious."

Noting his change of color, Kim was suddenly sympathetic to Dan's predicament. "Are you claustrophobic?"

"No, just opposed to being a sitting duck in a position where I'm unable to draw my gun. You can't believe Adams won't also be armed, can you? We'd both be vulnerable."

Kim huffed out a big sigh. "Good point, Dan. We have to keep thinking about this. There's got to be a way to catch him trying to do me harm so that he's locked up forever. Really, what's our alternative?"

— — — — — — — — — — — —

The drive to the cemetery in Terre Haute would take about ninety minutes according to Dan's map function. He opened the car door for Kim and settled in behind the wheel. She looked exhausted, her freshness from earlier in the morning having faded quickly.

"Why don't you ease the seat back and take a quick nap?" he asked. "The drive is flat and boring. You won't miss much."

"Believe me, I know the drive," Kim answered. "When my aunt was in the throes of her addiction, I drove Mom to 'the Haute' a lot. Mom hated I70, with good reason. It can be full of drivers who take unnecessary chances. Lots of times we'd sit at a standstill while wrecks were cleared. Even worse, we'd see the ambulances driving on the shoulder to pick up accident victims."

"Well, my internet map says the highway is green the whole way. You can sleep, and I recommend it. You think you're covering how tired you are, but you're not."

Kim chuckled and reclined her seat. "Busted," she said. "I'll close my eyes for just a bit."

According to Dan's dashboard clock, it took Kim all of three minutes to fall asleep. Her breathing became deep and regular. She seemed at peace as she slept. He hoped he could give her back that sense of freedom soon. He vowed Adams would be found quickly, as if his own life depended on it. And Kim's surely did.

Snaking over to Westlane and 71st street from Broad Ripple Village, Dan then took I465, the ring road around Indianapolis to the I70 exit. After stopping and slowing for the perennial work around the exits near Plainfield, he was finally able to gun the car to seventy miles per hour. He debated going over the limit since he was had an emergency car light he could attach to the car roof but decided Kim needed the extra few minutes of sleep. In addition, he enjoyed glancing at her beautiful face, even more enticing with its peaceful demeanor.

When she'd assumed fault for the end of her marriage, he'd hoped she would reveal a reason to end his absorption with her. Visions of her cheating on her husband with a patient, scamming the insurance companies, or cutting sessions short so she could cram in more billable hours gave him hope that his attraction to her would end. He was thinking about her too much, so much that even Anson noticed. Given Anson's usual cluelessness, that was a bad sign.

But Kim hadn't revealed any fatal flaws in her character. She had taken responsibility for Brad's loneliness which was ridiculous. If Dan had been the husband in that marriage, he would done the chores Kim mentioned and then enjoyed the free weekend time with her to the max. If she'd been too tired to talk at the end of the work-day, he'd have given her a massage to help her relax. He even would have learned to cook! Brad Newton was a fool to have let a woman like Kim go.

Newton was more than a fool, though. He was a thief, basically. Freeloading off Kim's first three years' earnings was despicable. What was wrong with family court judg-es? Their jobs were difficult, but wasn't it obvious who the wronged party in the Newton marriage was?

He also noted Kim hadn't said anything about Brad's infidelity. Again, Newton was a fool. Dan had his share of trysts in his history, sure. But if he were Kim's husband, there would be no one else. Never.

The drive was smooth, but Dan couldn't use his cruise control due to the many semi-trucks on the road. That was good. It made him pay attention to his driving with-out zoning out, while also allowing him to keep stealing glances at Kim's gorgeous face. Sleep was her only peace now. He vowed that would change as soon as possible. She deserved a better life than she had.

He doubted she'd agree. Knowing her personality, she'd tout all her blessings, all the ways God had given her favor. Her attitude seemed to be that Adams was just a trial to be endured, not a reflection of an unfair punishment from above. Dan wished he had some of that positive attitude. He was still smarting from his divorce, despite coming out relatively unscathed.

Just after the Greencastle exit, traffic ground to a complete stop. Checking his navigation map again, Dan was dejected to see a long line of red ink on the I70 path to Terre Haute. Using his patrol function, he learned a severe accident had happened at the Brazil on-ramp. They would be sitting on the highway for a while.

Kim stirred. "What's going on?"

"You seem to have predictive powers," Dan said. "Bad accident by Brazil."

"I hope no one is hurt. Our inconvenience is nothing compared to the suffering from a bad wreck. I've treated several accident survivors and their PTSD is real. And that's not counting any physical recovery they have to endure."

She closed her eyes and Dan knew she was praying. Kim Newton was a truly good person, almost a saint in his opinion. Despite all the agony in her life, she was praying for someone she'd never know.

"Does your faith really help you?" he asked.

"Sure does," Kim answered with a smile. "Adele wants me to go to her mega-church, but I've held her off. My little church is just right for me. Our pastor was very kind to me when my aunt died, and the other members came through for me, too." She looked out the window at the unending trail of cars. "Religion and faith are tricky, aren't they?"

Dan squirmed in his seat. "Not sure what you're getting at."

"I just mean that churches can lure us in with the hope they'll comfort, soothe, and celebrate with us as we live this crazy life. But often they disappoint, because they're made up of imperfect people, just like us."

"I see," Dan said.

"Enough deep talk," Kim said. "Look over there! Someone is roller blading on the highway shoulder!"

"Idiot," Dan grumbled. "That's another accident waiting to happen. When people become impatient, they start to drive on the shoulder to make up time."

"I wouldn't call him an idiot," Kim said. "I think he's just trying to make the best of a trying situation. Which is what we should do."

"What do you have in mind?" Dan smiled as he thought of several ideas about how to pass the time with Kim, but none of them were appropriate or feasible in his car. The tinted windows would provide cover, but still.

"I have a book on my phone. We could read aloud to each other."

"Really?" When he realized Kim wasn't kidding, he asked, "What's the book? Unless it's a thriller or mystery, I doubt I'd like it."

"You're worried it's a Jane Austin novel, aren't you?"

"As you said earlier, busted."

Kim laughed, a sound he wished he could hear every day. "It does happen to be the latest thriller from a best-selling author. Your only problem will be that you'll need to buy it after we get out of the jam and find out how it ends. I doubt we can read four-hundred pages in this sitting."

As he was about to agree with Kim, the driver in the car ahead of them left his car to walk his dog in the brush off the highway. He let the dog in the back seat and pounded the car roof in anger. Looking at Dan, he signaled his frustration with closed fists.

"Be right back," Dan said.

He looked at the man, five-feet-four if that much, a guy probably suffering from short-man syndrome. *I know psych stuff, too*, he thought. "Hey, buddy, this is tough, huh?"

The man smiled and extended his hand. "Billy Ray Jones," he said.

"Dan Westbrook," Dan replied. "You look like you're in a hurry."

"Yeah, my mother is in the Effingham, Illinois hospital and I'm going to be way late picking her up. That wouldn't be so bad, but my cell phone is out of juice."

Not wanting to let the man know he was a cop, which his department phone would reveal, Dan said, "Mine, too. Let me see if my girl has a phone you can use."

Calling Kim his "girl" wasn't quite the truth, but Dan could pretend. Hopefully she hadn't heard him. After his query, Kim readily agreed to loan Billy Ray her phone. His call was made to the hospital, he expressed his sincere thanks, and he returned to his car and dog.

"Your de-escalation techniques are good" Kim said. "Guys like that can get hot pretty quickly."

"I agree," Dan said. "He was ready to take his frustration out on someone. Thanks for your help."

"Nothing I wouldn't do for my guy," Kim said with a twinkle in her eye.

Dan's face was warm. "So, you heard?"

Kim's smile was answer enough.

"It was all part of my skilled de-escalation work to bond with Billy Ray," Dan said. "And it was effective, wasn't it?"

"Sure, Dan. Sure." Kim was still smiling

Dan knew he had to regroup, and fast. "Since we're not into reading aloud to each other, how else can we make this wait more tolerable? We've been here almost an hour."

"I'd like to know more about you," Kim said. "You know everything about me due to your investigation. What about you?"

"Not much to tell. You already know I'm divorced."

"Okay. What about your family? Are your parents living?"

Dan swallowed. "No. It's a sad story and one I still feel guilty about, though my sister says we did our best." He told Kim about his parents' accident and his regret that he didn't take their car keys.

"That's tough. I'm sorry for your loss, which I realize sounds trite. The two most important people in your life are gone and that's something that leaves a hole in your heart." Kim reached over and patted his hand, then clutched it in a gentle clasp. "For what it's worth, I agree with your sister.

You did your best. I've had clients whose kids took their keys away and they got another set from the dealer with a fabricated story. It happens."

Astounded by Kim's kindness, Dan reached over the kissed her cheek. She turned to him and put her hand on his face. Knowing he was in trouble but unable to stop himself, he kissed her softly, enjoying the feel of her lips on his. Kim leaned in and the kiss deepened.

It would have gotten deeper, but Billy Ray flashed his brake lights and waved a hand from his driver's side window. Cars began to inch along, signaling that at least one lane of the interstate had been cleared.

"Saved by your friend Billy Ray," Kim breathed. "I'm not sure if I'm happy or sad about it."

Dan laughed. "I'm sure about my feelings." He looked at her and winked. "Sad."

Flustered, Kim recovered enough to ask, "What about your decision to be a police officer? How did that come about?"

"It was in my blood. My father was a street cop back in the day. I saw what he dealt with. The good and the bad. But he was firm in his commitment to make Indianapolis a better place. I'm convinced he did."

"Did he ever get wounded in the line of duty?" Kim was twirling her hair, and Dan decided to believe her anxiety was reflecting her concern for him, not his dad.

"No, he was never shot. He did get roughed up several times but never landed in the hospital."

"That's good," Kim said. She looked at the cars ahead of them, clearly worried about something other than the accident victims. "What about you? Have you ever been shot?"

"A couple of times. Both minor grazes. No bullets left in my body, thank goodness."

"Yes, thank God," Kim breathed. "Like your dad, do you think you're making a difference? Are you making Indianapolis a better place?"

Dan thought a few seconds. "On my good days, I do. But other days I'm full of frustration. I remind myself it's not just Indy; most of the larger cities have the same issues we do."

"True. Our country is in a problematic place. But I have faith that the good people outnumber the bad. Things will even out."

Dan was now on firmer ground. He'd been wanting to ask Kim more about Russ Kellams. "Your friend Russ seems to be one of the good guys. Almost too good to be true."

Kim turned in her seat to face him. "What? You think Russ is involved in all this?"

"Just asking."

"He was stabbed! I got a concussion! He would never put me in danger, or his dog either!" Kim's frustration was evident as she searched for reasons Russ was innocent of Dan's suspicions. She was angry as well, her eyes darkening in a way Dan liked. He imagined they would darken when she was passionate about topics other than defense of a friend.

"Relax, Kim. I'm just asking," he repeated. "You have to admit Russ is almost the perfect man. He pays off the debts of his company, even though his partner was liable and responsible for most of them. He treats his ex-wife like a princess, even when she's pregnant quickly after their divorce. It's all a little unreal."

"Well, real or not, it's Russ. You don't know him, Dan. He's had a tragic life in many ways. It's none of your business, though."

Dan registered the put-down but plowed on. "Look, I need to identify everyone who's helping Adams. He's getting around much too easily. He has access to your movements and tracks you whenever he wants. Someone is helping him." Dan knew one helper was Angie Hess, but he wanted to be sure about Kellams.

"That someone isn't Russ," Kim said with a finality that indicated the discussion of Russ Kellams was over. "Instead of focusing on Russ, shouldn't you check further into the dialysis center? Adams spends lots of time there. He could be using treatment as an opportunity to make friends with more than one vulnerable accomplice." She looked out the window and leaned her head against the cool glass.

It was time to come clean. "As a matter of fact, Anson has already taken care of that. Turns out the head nurse might be involved with Adams. He works fast."

Shuddering, Kim looked at a mile marker as it flashed by. "We're almost to the exit for the cemetery. Take it and I'll guide you to the grounds." After a second, she said,

"I hope that woman is being careful. Tom could hurt her like he did me."

They rode in silence to the beautiful memorial grounds on the north side of Terre Haute. Kim told Dan where to park, grabbed the wreath she'd brought, and got out of the car before he could make it to her side.

Well, she's truly angry, he thought. Maybe for just reasons.

Knowing Kim shouldn't be by the burial plot on her own, he left the car and stood beside her. After she placed the large floral arrangement in its stand on the ground, Kim began to talk.

"My aunt was a hero in Viet Nam, as I told you," she said. "But her scars were internal and deep. Like many of the soldiers, she used drugs to self-medicate. Thankfully, she was discharged soon after she'd gotten into the worst of it. Once home, she was able to kick heroin, but alcohol became her substitute drug."

Dan was silent, waiting for more. Kim was almost in a place of her own as she remembered her aunt.

"Aunt Susan tried her best. And my mother did what she could. In fact, my parents paid for several stints in rehab. Eventually my father had enough."

"Those places are expensive. I get it," Dan said. He figured Kim's dad was comfortable but not made of money.

"Yes, lots of money down the tubes, as my dad used to say. I tried to educate him about the recidivism rate with addictions, and that each treatment stay leaves a little bit of health in its wake even if there's a relapse. Then my mother started in."

"Your mother?"

"She was convinced I could treat Aunt Susan. No amount of arguing about ethics, my lack of objectivity with a dear relative, or my lack of specialty training in addictions got through to her."

"What happened?" Dan asked. Kim had many layers, he was discovering. It wasn't enough that life had dealt her Brad Newton and Tom Adams, but to be guilted by her mother for her aunt's illness was almost too much.

"We were at an impasse. I consulted with an old professor. He agreed completely with me, that I should never try to treat my aunt. He even talked to my mom, telling her I could potentially do more harm than good for Susan."

Kim was silent. Dan ached for the beautiful woman next to him. Without realizing it, his arm was wrapped around her shoulders.

"Your prof was right, don't you think? I've seen enough of the addiction process to know it requires specialized treatment."

"Oh, he was right," Kim answered. "But it did little good. My mother was angry at me for months. Aunt Susan was upset by the rift between me and mom and began to drink even more."

Flustered, Dan looked at Kim. Her eyes were filling, but she was stiff with anger. "I'm sorry, Kim."

"You can guess the rest. Susan eventually died without any further treatment. My father's refusal to foot the bill for more inpatient stays, and my refusal to take her on as a client alienated my mother for months. Her grief over her sister's death was compounded by what she perceived as betrayals by those she loved most."

"Surely your mom came around," Dan said, hoping for the best. "Couldn't she have gone to Al-Anon meetings or something?"

"She repeatedly refused support groups of any kind. And no, she didn't come around. Part of the reason my parents retired to Florida was my supposed lack of loyalty to my aunt. My dad doesn't agree, of course, but he goes along with mom on all major decisions."

Dan ground his back molars. No one, especially Kim, deserved this kind of treatment from a parent. Guilt was a powerful emotion, as he well knew. Kim was still a captive, but she wasn't aware of its hold on her.

"Listen, Kim. You gave me some good advice about my parents and I'm going to try to return the favor. Just as my dad would have gotten car keys somehow, your aunt would also have found booze no matter what kind of treatment she was in. *She* had to be the one to take control of her life, not you. Your mother is way out of line."

Before he realized what he was doing, he had his arms around her, holding her close as she finally let the tears flow. As he rocked her in his arms, he absorbed her scent, a light floral he guessed, which suited her perfectly.

And again, before he knew what he was doing, his lips were on hers. Again.

Kim responded briefly but pulled away before he could deepen contact. "Thanks for your support about my mother," she whispered. "We need to get home."

"I guess we do. Maybe you can rest on the way back."

Kim nodded and returned to the car as she wiped her eyes. "We can go home now," she repeated. "I plan to sleep the whole way, so there's no need for us to talk."

CHAPTER TEN

KIM FEIGNED SLEEP FOR the first thirty minutes of the drive home. Dan's kiss had almost been her undoing. She wanted to stay in the comfort of his hug forever. The kiss had plenty of passion but also held the promise of deep caring, maybe love. No one had ever understood the complicated mess of her relationship with her parents better than Dan. She smiled as she remembered his attempt to empathize, which gradually gave in to his need to solve the problem. Typical guy, but she appreciated it. His suggestion of Al-Anon was a good one. Her mother, however, was too convinced of her superior understanding of what ailed her sister. In her opinion, Kim's supposed expertise was all that was required for a total cure of a devastating disease.

If that had been the case, Kim would have been happy to ditch all the ethical problems inherent in treating a close relative. But addiction, trauma, and longstanding character issues required more than a loving niece's counseling techniques. The rift with her mother would probably be permanent. Her father's weakness was long-standing as well. Dan's eyes had indicated he understood that painful reality. He'd lost both parents in a horrendous accident. He had an intimate acquaintance with the void of loss caused by stubborn natures.

The rides to Terre Haute and back were torture combined with bliss. Kim ached for Dan's comfort, but wondered at what his breach of police boundaries would cost him. Knowing Dan, he'd retreat as soon as he could. Kissing her was forbidden. He knew that but kissed her anyway. What did that mean?

Tired of her passive role is all of this mess, Kim opened her eyes. The exit sign for Greencastle few by, indicating at least another hour in the car with Dan. She decided to make him talk while they were trapped in the vehicle together.

"About that kiss," she opened.

Dan grimaced. "Yeah, I'm sorry."

"Sorry for what?" she countered. "I'm not sorry at all."

Sighing, Dan shifted in his seat while he passed a pickup truck loaded with an old mattress roped down with several connected bungee cords. "It was wrong. You know that. We had just discussed boundaries with your family. Then I went and breached *our* boundaries, big time."

"True. But I'm still not sorry." Kim gazed out at the flat Indiana corn fields and wondered briefly how long it would be before new housing developments took their place. But back to the matter at hand.

"Dan, I know you well enough to be sure that kiss was based on real feelings. It wasn't a casual boundary breach. What's going on with us?"

"Nothing. There can't be anything between us, Kim."

Pleased at the sadness in Dan's voice, Kim pushed on. "I'm not some inexperienced teenager, Dan. I know a passionate kiss when I get one." She smiled at him, but he stared ahead at the flat interstate. "You're ignoring my response."

Dan waited her out. Fine, she'd say it.

"I was passionate, too. I'm starting to care for you. I look forward to our awkward conversations. I want Adele to go home. I want to be alone with you."

At the mention of Adele vacating Kim's home, Dan smiled. "Okay, I'll admit I've hoped Adele would need to do laundry or pay a few bills at her place."

They laughed together, easing the tension a bit, then Dan continued. "Even so, I can't let my attraction to you continue, Kim. If things get messy between us, the investigation will be compromised. Someone could get hurt. I can't let that happen."

"The investigation might be *better* if we were open about our feelings," Kim said. "It might make us more efficient and innovative as we think about ways to trap Adams."

"Trust me, that's not how it works."

Kim digested Dan's comment. So, he'd been involved with victims before? Was he more of a player than she realized? Did Dan enjoy being the knight-in-shining armor for the women he protected?

They were silent for the rest of the trip. She was a lovesick fool, and she'd misread all of Dan's signals. When they pulled up to her house, she was out of the car as soon as it stopped. She entered the house, greeted Adele, and went to her home office without speaking to Dan. She had to focus on her patients. There was absolutely no point in thinking about the wonder of Dan's kisses.

- - - - - - - - - - - - - -

After Kim went to her study to meet with her telehealth appointments for the evening, Dan continued to generate some sort of plan that wouldn't get him laughed out of headquarters. He began with a prayer of thanks that he hadn't interviewed Adams at the elder care facility currently housing him. Adams probably didn't know what he looked like, which would give him a small advantage. But he still had to hide in the cramped RV. Kim said it was the largest model currently in production, but it was hellishly small for his needs. And he hadn't admitted it, but he *was* a little claustrophobic.

Her idea of removing the sofa bed had some merit, but he'd be stiff, lacking the agility needed to get the jump on Adams when the time came. Adams was sure to be armed, so Dan had to be quick. Where else could he hide? Using his phone, he pulled up sample floor plans of large RVs. Fundamentally, they weren't all that different from each other. The sofa bed option was the best he could find based on the plans he saw.

Drifting away from planning, Dan was appalled again at the cost of the vehicles. A million dollars was low end for most Class A models. Who would pay that kind of money for something on wheels when it could buy oceanfront property? Okay, a small condo in a high-rise on the beach, but something that would appreciate instead of losing a chunk of the investment as it rolled off the lot. He was having happy fantasies of living on the beach with Kim when he noticed the refrigerators in the RV plans.

Many were full-size. Plenty of room for him to hide standing up at a crouch, if they could fashion a false front, or gut the interior. Would Adams think to look in the refrigerator when he examined the space? If Kim allowed Adams to overtake her, he might be excited enough to forego a thorough search. And if Adams took Kim's gun (which Dan planned to be empty of ammunition), he might just enjoy the capture enough to assume he'd won the battle for control of her and be careless in his search of the vehicle.

Then the tricky part would begin. Dan would have to wait in the fridge until Adams threatened Kim, or worse case, began to strip or beat her. His stomach turned at the thought of her being injured again, or God forbid, mortally wounded.

First things first. He'd have to float this plan to Kim and Anson and get their approval. Then they would have to tell Russ Kellams he'd need to remove his refrigerator. Would Russ know anyone who could fashion a false front? It couldn't be that difficult, could it?

Dan shuddered. The truly horrendous part was putting Kim in danger again. The woman was under his skin in a big way. Her beauty, smarts, and unwillingness to concede defeat to Tom Adams caused him to respect and value her. But it was more than that. He could care for a woman like this. That Adams had almost raped her made him gag. And that would be Adams's goal this time. He'd rough Kim up enough to make her subservient, then use his anger and deviant view of the world to get her naked. Then his fun would begin.

He knew he was too involved and too invested in Kim to know if his thinking was sound. Realizing he would want to be with Kim if the circumstances were different, he knew he had to run this by Anson. If the plan was stupid, Anson would tell him. Anson was smart and maybe he would come up with something better. Another plus for Anson was that he wasn't dreaming about living on the beach with Kim. He sent a quick message to his partner.

Anson responded to his text immediately. They made arrangements for a supper meeting. He'd tell Adele and Kim to expect a guest for dinner. At that moment, Kim appeared in the living room.

"You're early, Dr. Newton. I thought you were booked until after eight."

"My last client had to work overtime. Since money is tight for him, I totally understand." Kim stretched and arched her back, which Dan enjoyed in spite of himself. "And I'm tired from our trip today, so I'm not arguing."

"I'm sorry about your client, but glad you don't have to work so late," Dan said.

"When I came in, you looked troubled, Detective," she said. "I can't imagine what's the matter." She rolled her eyes at her sarcasm and added, "I haven't thanked you enough for your help today. You deserve my unending appreciation for listening to me talk about my aunt."

Her unending appreciation was one thing, but Kim was ignoring the important parts of their afternoon. Dan hoped for more, in a world where Adams was in jail for good. Or not breathing ever again. A world where he and Kim could be more than a victim and a cop. Not that she was a passive victim. Not at all. She was tough. And he was in deep.

"I hope you and Adele are up for some company tonight," he said. "My partner, Anson Yeager, is coming for a late dinner. Four heads are better than three, and all that. Anson has the heartbeat of headquarters, too. He'll know what kind of plan will get approved."

"No problem," Adele said from the kitchen. "I've got plenty of pasta for one extra. Does your friend have any food allergies? Or vegan tendencies?"

Dan laughed. "Adele, you sound like you'd convert him if he did have such unacceptable tendencies. But no, Anson will eat about anything."

"Good," the crusty old woman answered. "You might warn him, though, that my spaghetti sauce is laced with enough garlic to kill a vampire. Or a werewolf. Or a zombie. Whatever the legend says. It's the best."

- - - - - - - - - - - - - -

Anson Yeager, true to his Amish roots, was an aficionado of home cooking. Dan shook his head at his partner as he almost licked the pasta plate. Yeager was embarrassing himself. "Anson, Kim has a dishwasher," he said. "No need for you to clean the dish on your own."

Swiping the plate with his last remnant of garlic bread, Anson smiled. "You have no idea how long it's been since I've had good cooking. Adele, you are a true artist." Finishing off the crusty piece of bread, he continued. "And let no one criticize the amount of garlic in your sauce. It's perfect."

Adele laughed. "You sound like my late husband. It was his Sicilian grandmother's recipe, not that she ever approved of me. I was lucky to get a copy of it before she passed. But my hubby was grateful that I continued his family's tradition."

"Would you share the recipe with my girlfriend?" Anson asked.

"No, never for just a girlfriend. Why not you?" Adele shot back. Her feminist orientation was surprisingly strong for a woman of her generation and cultural roots. "You are just as capable of cooking as your girl is."

"Correct," Anson replied. "I'd be honored to make the recipe."

"I'll send you a screen shot," Adele said as she scrolled through her phone's recipe file. "You're welcome."

The group chuckled, grateful for the reprieve from the purpose of the meeting. No work had been done while they ate, but now was the time.

"We need to figure out how to trap Adams without Kim getting hurt. Or me getting hurt, for that matter," Dan began. "Part of me hates the idea of using the RV as our setting, but in a way it's a good idea."

Arching her brows, Kim asked, "What? You said it was a fiasco waiting to happen. I remember you using the word 'ridiculous' several times."

"Yes, because it's such a bad idea, I think Adams could be lulled into a false sense of safety. He'll think he has you completely trapped. After he searches the RV, he'll be sloppy with you, enjoying your fear. Our problem is where to hide me."

Dan munched on the last piece of bread. Swallowing, he added, "The refrigerator intrigues me. Is there any way we could fashion a false appliance? Like a real door, but on a plywood shell painted to look like stainless steel?"

Anson, the handy man of the police force, shook his head. "Dan, it will look too obvious and fake. Adams is smart, as we've said, and he'll notice right away. Knowing him, he'll fill the appliance full of bullets to add to Kim's horror. He'll get off on that, for sure."

Dan frowned and admitted Anson was right. "So where should I hide? We've already determined that outside or under the vehicle is too risky. It's got to be inside."

"Wait a sec," Kim said. She tapped her phone screen a few times and showed the group what she'd found.

"These faux appliances are often used in demo RVs. Buyers usually have preferences for high end ranges and what-not, so they order their own after purchase. They're obviously fake, so Adams won't question their presence." Her eyes glistened for a moment. "He could still shoot the facade full of holes, though. I'd hate to see that happen, Dan."

Dan wanted to wrap Kim in his arms and soothe her unshed tears. He knew Anson was watching him, so he gathered himself. "Me too," he grunted. "No one is going to get hurt, trust me. We just need a good approach."

The group kept discussing the option of pseudo appliances as they ate their dessert. Kim had made a cheesecake from scratch before her nap yesterday. The woman could cook as well as she could handle a potential murderer. Dan wondered about his own future safety, not at Adams's hands but in terms of his heart being wide open to Kim.

"Hello, Detective," Kim said. "Where'd you go?"

"Just thinking," Dan said. Anson grinned, knowing what was up. Dan would have to keep him quiet. "What if we sold tickets to the RV demo? Or if we had a metal detector at the door?"

Anson frowned. "A metal detector gives it away and scares good people. And to be fair to Russ Kellams, it ruins his chance to showcase his design skills. People would be really turned off."

"True," Adele said. "But the ticket idea has potential. I've often had to buy a ticket for various Indy decorator showhouses or parades of homes in new neighborhoods. They want your name and email address to build their subscription lists."

The trio looked at Adele in wonder. *My ageism strikes again*, Dan thought.

"That's a great idea," Kim gushed. "Surveying the guest list would be easy." She drummed her fingers on the table. "Of course, Adams won't give his real name. He might even be in disguise."

"You've seen him in the flesh, and we haven't. Recently, in fact," Dan observed. "What are his features like up close? What sort of disguises could he wear?"

Kim startled and looked away, as if the memory of Tom's face was literally painful. It probably was. Nonetheless, she shored up some ideas. "He's handsome, as psychopaths often are," she said. "A real golden boy, with blonde hair and blue eyes that almost sparkle. And his features are refined, almost delicate. He could pretend to be younger than his actual age." She blinked hard and added, "My goodness, he could even disguise himself as a woman without much effort. He's tall, but slim. Maybe this isn't a good idea. What if we miss him and he gets in before you're there, while I'm alone?"

In an attempt to quiet Kim's panic, Dan placed his hand over hers. Ignoring Anson's surprise, he said, "You will never be alone in that RV. I'll be there with you, no matter what."

"You'd better be," Adele said with a hard glare in Dan's direction. "I've got another idea. What if I was in the RV, too? I could pass out the hors d'oeuvres that Russ always provides at open houses, or make sure no one uses the nonfunctional bathroom."

This idea led to more talk of the plan's merits and risks. Kim rose to get the group more iced tea. "Before we move further, we've got to get Russ's permission. If he's not on board, we have no plan at all."

"Oh, we've got a plan," Dan muttered. "Russ will be cooperative." He didn't trust Russ, despite all Kim's positive input about the man.

Anson laughed. "Calm down, Dan. It will all come together. Kim's got a point. Russ could actually help flesh out our thoughts. He might have better ideas for hiding your unusually large mass."

Kim called Russ, put him on speaker, and asked him to come over after breakfast tomorrow. He agreed but was annoyed when she wouldn't give him details. "What's up, Kim? I have a right to know."

"You'll know tomorrow," Dan replied. "It's better if we talk in person."

The planning session fizzled out after the call to Russ. Everyone was emotionally spent. On the front porch, Dan thanked Anson for his help, and for his willingness to return tomorrow.

"It's okay, buddy. We'll get this creep." They shook hands and Anson added, "Nothing will happen to your girlfriend. Don't worry."

Dan thought about denying the "your girlfriend" part of Anson's message, but said, "Not my girlfriend, Anson. Not yet at least."

CHAPTER ELEVEN

RUSS SHOWED UP AT nine the next day as planned, carrying a large box from Long's Bakery. Kim had two of her favorite traditional yeast donuts, while the others had fun sampling the frosted and filled concoctions. Adele and Anson debated the merits of whipped-cream versus pudding-filled, with Adele winning for cream based on her lifetime of experience. Sugar-sated and optimistic, the group began to talk.

After hearing the latest in the situation involving Adams, Russ weighed in. "Hiding Dan is our biggest challenge. The RV is big, but efficient with storage. Dan, you could fit easily into the rear storage area, where folks keep ATVs, bikes, and so on. But you'd have no entry to the main living area without leaving storage and getting in through the front door."

"What if Dan was in the vehicle storage area, and somehow we could signal him when Adams arrives?" Adele asked. "I could leave my cell phone line open to Dan's and use a code word when we spot Adams."

"That could work," Russ said. "Even if Adams locks the front door, I have extra keys for Dan and Anson to use."

"This solves the problem of Adams shooting up the false appliances," Kim said. "He'll do it anyway to scare me, I'm sure. I worry about Adele, though." She looked at her friend. "You're going to be in Adams's way. He'll either hurt you before he starts on me, or make you watch, or both. I don't like putting you at risk."

"Let me decide," Adele said. "You've been there for me, Kimmy, countless times. All those rides to the doctor, nursing me through the chemo, listening to me sob and vent when my husband died. This is what friends do for each other."

Dan and Anson shared a look of concern, knowing this risk was more than the average friendship required. "Adele, I'm going to be blunt," Anson said. "Your life could end in this scenario. We know Adams loves to torture people. He could kill you outright just to enjoy Kim's pain at witnessing your death. Or he could kill you slowly as he relishes Kim's agony. Are you really ready for that possibility?"

The group was silent. After a few seconds, Dan, Anson, and Kim looked at Adele. Russ simply shook his head and mouthed, "No."

"I'm as ready to die as the next person. More so, probably. I'm eighty-five years old, and I've had a good life. Let's do this."

"You may be ready, but I'm not," Kim said. "Adele, you're precious to me. There's no way I'm risking your life in the RV. You've got to stay away."

The group ate more donuts as they tried to flesh out the plan to trap Adams. Russ agreed to sell tickets online instead of offering open admission, saying he'd put a note on his website. "It will probably help me in the long run," he said. "It makes viewing the RV look more exclusive."

"And sales should close at least two days before the event," Dan said. "We'll need time to do background checks on the attendees. If we come up with suspicious names or email addresses, we'll be better prepared."

"When should you enter the storage area, Dan? Early that morning? Or the night before?" Kim pressed her temples as she thought. "That sounds horrible, though. Waiting in that dark storage area all night."

"I've handled worse," Dan replied with a smile. He pretended to himself for what seemed like the tenth time that he wasn't a bit claustrophobic. "The night before is definitely the way to go. Anson, I want you to register for a ticket as well. If Adams shows and is recognized by Kim or Russ, you can enter before the place empties out."

"Done and done," Anson said.

"It's still so tenuous," Kim wailed. "I'll bet Adams has a cop detector wired into his sick brain. He'll know I won't be unprotected."

Adele licked the powdered sugar off her lips. "You're right, Kimmy. He'll be hoping you have help. He'll laugh at my presence, and maybe that will lower his guard. He'll probably frisk me." She shuddered at the thought. "I could provide plenty of opposition, and the guys will hear that on my open phone. But will he think I'm the only helper on site?"

"I thought we covered this," Kim said. "You're not going to be there, Adele."

"We'll see." The elderly woman sipped her tea, looking subdued.

Kim knew better but kept silent.

"Russ, what about your presence?" Dan asked. "Is Kim usually there when you're showing the RV?"

"Of course," Russ said. "Kim and I are a team. Basically, we show the place together and also provide each other with break time or the chance to retrieve stuff from our cars as needed."

Knowing he would hurt Adele's feelings, Dan continued. "So, we may not need you, Adele. Russ can be Kim's backup. I hate putting you at risk."

Adele stiffened. "I want to be there, Dan. It's not unheard of to have three in the RV to help with the 'Looky-Loos.' Sometimes Kim has to stand at the door so there won't be too many people in the RV at once."

Knowing he was beaten in this round, Dan regrouped. "Fine, all three of you can be there. Just hear me say you will all be at risk for injury or death. Understood?"

Everyone nodded. After a moment of thick silence, Kim said, "Let's summarize. Dan will be in the RV storage area the night before. Prior to opening to the public, we'll search the RV for Adams. He's likely to break in early and hide. If he's not there, Russ and I will handle the day as we usually would. Adele will hand out food and monitor the bathroom. If we spot Adams, Adele will say the code phrase, which I think should be 'checkered flag,' and Dan will exit the storage area and come to arrest Adams. Anson will help, since he'll be in the RV posing as a guest. No problems, right?"

Dan and Anson looked at each other again. Each knew this was a terrible plan, full of uncertainties and holes through which Adams could have free reign to kill them all.

"Yeah, no problems, Kim. None at all."

"Quit patronizing me," Kim said. "We know it's a horrendously bad plan. But it's all we've got. Going back to Adams's ultimate goal, which is to exact revenge on me for testifying and sending him to prison, this is our best shot. I refuse to be imprisoned in my home for the next several months while he manages to get another medical release in order to get me. We've got to do this now."

More silence resulted, as everyone thought about the possibilities if and when something went wrong. Adele finally spoke.

"Dan, we've talked about not being armed with guns, since Adams could easily take them from Kim or me. What about other weapons?"

Dan bristled but Anson stepped in. "Adele, you've got a point. Think about it, Dan. There are gel pepper spray units we could disguise as small fire extinguishers. The department just bought several flashlights that are also stun guns. And IMPD purchased a few police batons that we could modify to look like a cane for Adele." He studied

Adele, and added, "If you don't mind, that is. You'd have to stoop a little, so you'd look like you needed the cane."

"Speaking of patronizing," Adele said, wincing a little. "But I'd be happy to stoop even more than usual if it will get that man out of Kim's life."

"Okay, we have a bad plan, but with some defense built in," Dan said. "Now we have to generate all the possible ways the plan could play out. More specifically, we have to think like Adams. How will he approach the RV? What will he be thinking?"

Two hours later, they thought they'd covered all the possibilities. Dan knew they hadn't, but they'd done the best they could.

They were about to adjourn when Russ said, "Kim, we need to go to the antique mall in Plainfield before we finalize the RV décor. I'm in need of a few more tchotchkes. You know me, things need to be perfect but unpredictable."

"Sure, Russ. I'm surprised I hadn't remembered that. We always go picking before the grand opening of your spaces. What do you have in mind?"

"Colorful pieces, of course. Playful but sophisticated. Suitable for high-end buyers, but also within reach of a person wanting to refresh their own home."

Russ's comments could have been gibberish as far as Dan was concerned. Playful but sophisticated? How was that possible? What in the world was a *tchotchke*? More to the point, the outing was a potential disaster, and he made his feelings plain.

"Not happening, Russ. We can't let Kim leave the house, even if I'm with her. I would assume the antique mall is a crowded space full of places for Adams to hide or flee. Who knows what he'll do with this opportunity?"

Noting the familiar stubborn set to Kim's beautiful face, he looked to Anson for support. No help was coming from his partner's direction. "You're asking for our plan to be over before it starts, Kim. Adams could take you and have you for himself before you'd bought the first tchotchke."

Anson finally weighed in. "Dan is right. Public spaces, crowds of people, and easy exits are your worst nightmares, Kim."

Everyone leaned in as they watched Kim. She finally spoke. "You two make good points. But I think we could use this shopping trip to our advantage. Since we know Adams is watching me somehow, it could give him a sense of power when he sees me away from the house. Maybe it will lower his guard, thinking we're unaware of his ability to get to me."

"Doubtful," Dan said.

"Can I be tracked if he does grab me?"

"There are ways, yes," Dan answered. "Adams will be savvy to them all, though. Remember, this is a guy who's beaten his ankle monitor."

"Okay. What else can we do to ensure my safety?" Kim thought for a second. "I've got it! Russ and I will walk arm-in-arm or hold hands. Right, Russ? You're my new boyfriend."

Dan didn't like the sound of this, though for reasons less related to safety than to Kim having a man other than him in her life. Luckily, her new plan was as flawed as her idea for tracking. "It sounds very cozy, but Adams will be able to separate you two in an instant. And based on what I know of you and Russ, you'll separate on your own the minute you see something for the RV in the distance."

To Dan's surprise, Kim laughed. "You're right, Dan. Once we spot a true find, we hustle over to get if before someone else does. This once, though, I think Russ and I could show some restraint and make sure we look at everything together."

Dan knew he'd lost this argument. Maybe Kim had a point. It wouldn't hurt if Adams became too confident. That's when criminals made their biggest mistakes. He nodded and said, "I give. You and Russ have to swear to stay arm-in-arm. And Anson and I will be around, in disguise. You'll have two hours to do your shopping, then it's right back to Broad Ripple, right?"

- - - - - - - - - - - - - -

Anson left for the office. After a few minutes of cleaning the powdered sugar and frosting off every surface, Adele said her goodbyes as well, promising to be back soon. Dan said he needed to go to his place to gather a few more items of clothing, though Kim was sure he was getting weapons or whatever police needed for a plan like theirs. He moved to the front door.

"Hold on, Dan," Kim said. "Now that I'm revived by our plan to trap Adams, I want to finish our conversation about what happened at the gravesite." She knew she was being a bit demanding, but Dan was worth it. And he sure wasn't going to take the lead.

"There's nothing to finish," Dan grumbled. "I told you I was out of line, period. Enough said."

Kim moved closer to him. She could see his knuckles whiten as he gripped the doorknob. Her hand on his cheek, she whispered, "You feel it, too. I know it. I'm not just a weak victim to you."

He was silent, then took her hand in his.

Kim led them to the sofa and took a deep breath. "Dan, once this is over, I want us to explore what we have. I've had my fill of weak, manipulative men. You're different, and I want to know you better. Can't we plan on that? Plan on seeing where our attraction leads us when we're free of Adams?"

She saw the doubt in his eyes and the truth nearly knocked the wind from her lungs. Dan didn't view her as a victim, he thought of her as another part of his past.

"I'm not your ex-wife, Dan. I'm my own person, woman who is very attracted to you. I'm humiliating myself here, but I'll be fine if you don't want me."

After widening his eyes when Kim mentioned his ex, Dan didn't respond. Kim knew she'd gone too far. This man would do the honorable thing, which unfortunately meant he'd drop her the second Adams was behind bars.

They sat, looking at each other in silence. Then Dan caressed her face and lowered his lips on hers.

"I'm a fool," he muttered after their long kiss.

Kim caught her breath and smiled. "You're not a fool," she said. "You just can't resist my many charms."

Their laughter eased the happy tension.

"I'll be back soon," he said.

Kim locked up after him and felt an aching loneliness at the lack of his presence. She was also left completely alone with her spiraling fears.

What if her dear friends were injured or worse? It would be her fault. Adele was more frail than she admitted, with severe arthritis and lingering effects of the chemo. Russ was a healthy middle-aged man, but he was no warrior. Not to mention his stab wound. How could Kim deal with putting them in danger?

They seemed to be willing, though. She knew they loved her. Deep down, she recognized this whole mess wasn't her fault, either. Tom Adams was a sick criminal, one obsessed with revenge.

But what about Anson and Dan? They could also be hurt or killed. Kim's focus centered primarily on Dan. He cared for her; she could tell. Did she have feelings for him? Yes. His gruff demeanor hid a scarred, even tender, inner world. His empathy at the gravesite was proof of his past pain. There was something more, though. He was intelligent, strategic, and focused on getting her to a place where she could live a safe, normal life. Did she want to be part of that life? She guessed he did.

Jarring her out of her dreamy fantasy, her cell phone rang. The "unknown caller" phrase displayed. Kim thought about letting it go to voicemail but wondered if Dan was calling from a protected line. She answered.

"Hey there, Dr. Kim," the deep voice resonated. "How's it going with your old lady neighbor and your cop friends?"

Kim caught her breath and gasped out a sob. Before she could speak, the caller continued.

"When are you going to realize I'm always with you?" Adams taunted. "I was with you in the ED at the hospital, I've watched your two saviors try to ruin my friendship with my dialysis nurse, and even prejudice the boss at my current place of living. And you should close your curtains. You and the head cop are getting a little cozy for my taste. Gotcha." Then the line went dead.

After crying for a few minutes, Kim gathered herself. Adams was watching her house. He could be ready to invade her precious space and do terrible things to her. She was vulnerable, despite all the planning Dan, Anson, and Adele had done. Looking around for weapons, she picked up an old golf club of her father's, along with a canister of cooking spray. That deviant would feel some pain before he hurt her. She was no match for a real weapon. And Adams was sure to have one.

Her back-door lock tumbled. She stood behind the shelves in the mudroom, hidden by a coat rack loaded with her walking hats and jackets. A man stepped in. She sprayed his face full of butter-flavored spray and made ready to swing her dad's putter.

CHAPTER TWELVE

"GOOD GRIEF, WOMAN!" DAN yelled. "What are you doing?"

Stopping in time so that Dan was spared a chip shot to the head, she stared at him and winced as her weapon clattered on the tiled floor. "It's you. Thanks for coming back. I was afraid you wouldn't."

After rubbing his teary eyes for several seconds, he asked, "What's going on? Why did you attack me?" Dan stepped closer and enveloped her in his arms. "You're shaking. It's the post-adrenaline crash." He looked at her closely and said, "He called you, didn't he?"

"He sure did. He's watching us, Dan. He knew you, Anson, Russ, and Adele were here. He knows you and Anson are cops and that Adele is my neighbor. He suggested I draw my curtains because he got an eyeful of us carrying on. How long has he been stalking me?" She began to cry again but made an effort to stop. "I've got to be brave. If he gets to me, I'll be even more vulnerable." Kim realized she was being held by Dan, which was very nice, but had to stop. She wiggled out of his embrace.

Shaking his empty arms, Dan shrugged. "He's been at this for a while," he admitted. "It's on me that I didn't anticipate his presence." He stopped, lost in generating several scenarios. "We could use this to our advantage, but how? I can't figure out how he's watching you while in an assisted living facility. Granted, the administrator is useless in terms of monitoring Adams, but he's got help of some kind. Someone is giving him rides, money, and obviously surveillance equipment."

Dan was reminding her about the likely culprit. Kim was appalled that a nurse would fall for Adams's charms so easily. But she also knew how powerful loneliness was in terms of clouding a person's judgment. She'd married Brad, after all.

Kim's eyes dilated and she struggled to breathe. "He's watching me electronically? Is my home bugged or worse? Can he film me when I'm showering or dressing? That was his goal last time." She covered her mouth and tried not to gag. "To record me naked and have his way for the camera."

Dan led Kim to the couch and sat beside her. "No, your home is safe. We checked it for bugs and cameras the day we arrived. I didn't tell you but that's my mistake." Dan held her hand. "The house is secure, but outside there's probably a camera few houses away to watch our comings and goings. It's easy technology these days."

Ignoring the rush that Dan's touch had caused, Kim gathered her thoughts. That pervert Adams had no business spying on her. "Then let's find it and destroy it!" she shouted.

"No, let's keep his equipment in place," Dan said. "He'll think he's got the upper hand."

Kim nodded, hand on her mouth again. Slowly the fire returned to her soul. She was sick of Adams and his games. "I can't call him back, but I could message him in a different way. What if I stood outside the house and pointed to my phone? He'd call me back, I'm sure."

"Good idea, but what do you want to talk to him about?" Dan propped his feet on the coffee table with a thud. "No, it's better if you don't talk. Let him control the conversation. Act scared, upset, and when he lets you speak try to bargain. Tell him Adele can't be harmed but you'll do whatever he wants. Emphasize that you're tired of being scared and that you can be his friend. Feed him some garbage about you misdiagnosing him and how sorry you are."

"Don't you think he'll see right through that? He knows I hate him."

"True, but he's coming to the point of full-on delusions. Right, Kim? You're the shrink, not me."

"Maybe," Kim said. "But he's smart, Dan. He'll know I'm lying."

"That could work for us, too," Dan said with a smile. "Adams will think he's pulled one over on you by making you lie in desperation. He'll go along with you to lure you in."

Kim looked at Dan, enjoying his handsome face as it creased in concentration. He seemed to care about her, more than if she were just another victim needing his protection. If only that were true. She could have a future with someone like him. Someone exactly like him, smart and dedicated to his mission to help others.

Dan continued, oblivious to her silence. "I've got a new plan. Why don't you offer Adams a sneak peak of the RV? Make arrangements to meet him a couple of hours before it opens to ticket holders. This will keep Adele safe, and I can still be hidden in the storage area the night before. Russ won't have to be there either."

"We've accounted for the safety of Russ and Adele. That's good. But I'm still scared, Dan."

"Good. If you weren't, I'd be worried. Let's plan for tonight first. I'm going to stay until it's late. I'll make a show of leaving. After thirty minutes, you go out to the porch and stand under the light. Circle around like you're looking for Adams. Bring out your phone, point to it and go inside. My bet is he'll call within a few minutes."

Kim nodded. The fire in her spirit was still burning. With Dan's help, she'd get this creep out of her life. It had to be done. She was up to it.

- - - - - - - - - - - - -

Kim watched Dan leave a little after eleven-thirty, without a wave or a backward glance at her. She hoped Tom would be surprised her IMPD friend wasn't staying the night. Surely he would know there would be surveillance on the house. She sent a quick prayer up to the heavens, imploring God to let Adams be lulled by a false sense security, a belief that Kim thought she was in no danger from him.

Taking a deep breath, Kim opened the front door. She swiveled slowly as she looked up and down her street, seeming to search for Adams. Then she pointed to her phone and went inside.

The four-minute wait seemed like an eternity. Her phone rang, the "Unknown Caller" label displayed, and she answered.

"Really?" Tom's voice asked. "You *wanted* me to call? This is obviously a trap, Dr. Kim. You want to play? I just can't resist."

Using her soft, soothing voice, she said, "Tom is this you?"

"Of course it is, Dr. Kim. What do you want to talk about? Did your cop friend devise a plan to trap me? You know it's not going to work."

"No, he's useless," Kim said. "He's gone for the night because I made him leave. I can't stand being talked down to all the time. And that made me think of you in a backwards way. I did that with you, didn't I? I'm sorry, really I am."

Tom's breathing became more shallow, but he seemed pleased. "Dr. Kim don't try to snow me. You're not sorry at all. I'm a prisoner because of you and you like it."

"No, Tom, I mean it. I reviewed my ED assessment of you with a colleague after it was all over. It's called peer supervision. Anyway, she told me I missed a lot. I pegged you as a super handsome narcissist before I listened to your story, your pain. I'm ready to go to the authorities and try to get your sentence shortened to time served. I think that's what they call it. Dan Westbrook, the cop you've seen, is really angry with me and left in a huff." Kim took a few deep breaths as if to calm herself, and added, "Please, call me Kim, Tom. None of this Dr. Kim stuff. We need to talk like friends."

"Dr. Kim, you can't expect me to buy this flimsy tale. How sorry can you be?" He paused and added, "Of course, you could prove yourself to me. That would help."

Kim could hear the excitement in his voice, the slight tremor as he formed his words. "What can I do?" she pleaded. "Really, I need to make this right."

Tom stuttered as he said, "You and I need to meet, alone. In a private place with no one watching or listening. And I'll know if they are. It will go badly for your old lady friend if you lie to me."

Kim choked back a tearful protest. "No! You can't hurt Adele. She's been like family to me through all this." After a lull, Kim added, "In fact, she told me I was wrong about you. She said you had feelings for me that I missed. Feelings that were separate from a normal client-therapist relationship. She also took your side when I didn't admit you to the hospital that night. Adele always calls me a hard-hearted person." Kim screwed her eyes shut as she continued to lie.

"Adele's got that right," Tom said. "You've been quite the shrew, Kim. I'll let it go for now, though. When can we meet?"

"Not tonight, but I wish we could," Kim said softly, nearly gagging at her words. "They're watching, which you know. Maybe at the RV on race day, before anyone is there? Would that work?"

"It might," Adams hedged. "It's a few days off, though. I'll have to generate a crisis medical appointment to get out of this place. You'd better be alone, Dr. Kim. No tricks or funny stuff."

"No tricks," Kim said. "It's time for us to talk, to get to know each other. The RV will be empty until at least nine in the morning. General admission starts at ten. Maybe after we meet and you've slipped away, we can get some breakfast. I'll tell Russ I've got a migraine or something. He'll let me go with no fuss."

"Fine, we'll start with a meeting in the RV. Race day is Sunday, right?"

Everyone in Indiana knew the race was on Sunday, but Kim thought Adams was trying to act confused so she would trust him more. As if that would ever happen.

When she paused to reply, he added, "You shrinks are good actresses, Kim. There's no way you'll meet me and then go to breakfast. Your end goal is to put me back in jail. Admit it."

Kim sighed, as if she were digging deep to make Adams trust her. And she was digging deep, no doubt about it. She had to convince him he had her support, despite her aversion to his very presence on earth.

"Not anymore, Tom. As I said, my peer supervisor said I missed a lot with you. That's why I settled the lawsuit. You deserved better, and I'm going to make sure you're released soon."

Adams hooted. "Whatever, Kim. As I said, the race is Sunday. Can't we meet before that?"

"No, not before Sunday. We'll all be there Friday and Saturday setting up, so those days are out. Russ is a perfectionist so after we get everything placed, we'll be dusting and making sure things are up to his standards."

"I'll see you Sunday morning at eight," Adams said. "If this is a trap, I'll kill the old lady. Have no doubts that I'll get to her. Got it, Dr. Kim?"

Kim sobbed. "No, don't hurt anyone, Tom. It's all my fault, not Adele's or anyone else's. I was stupid and caught up in my own sense of power when you came to the emergency department. I was also annoyed that I'd been summoned in the middle of the night. I'm the one you want to punish."

Kim stared at the dead phone. That jerk had ended the call when she was mid-sentence. She was filled with disgust at her false groveling to Adams and at his cruelty. He was beyond mentally ill. While they'd talked, she felt true evil emanating from the phone.

Did she believe in such evil? Weren't we all God's children? Had some unknown childhood experience ruined Tom Adams forever? Or had he been infected in some other way with the devil's spirit? She wasn't a theologian. All she could do was pray for her safety and that of everyone on the case. She knew she should pray for Adams as well but couldn't bring herself to ask God to help him. What she wanted to pray for was Adams's punishment. It would be a selfish prayer, serving only her desire to exit this nightmare as quickly as possible.

Her phone buzzed again. Could Adams be calling back? Assuming the demeanor of a woman who was afraid (which wasn't too difficult) and contrite, she answered. "Hello? Tom is that you? I was hoping you'd call again."

"Kim, it's me," Dan said. "I'm at the back door. Let me in." Dan entered the house for the second time that night and studied Kim's tense shoulders. "Sounds like you've talked to our deluded friend. What did he have to say?"

"Quite a lot," Kim answered. "We're going to meet alone in the RV on race day at eight in the morning. I said I could fake a migraine or something if he wanted to go to breakfast afterward. He said if I try to trick him, he'll kill Adele." She filled Dan in on the particulars of the conversation and added, "I have a feeling he won't show, Dan. He's going to try to get me with people around. A crowd will give him better cover. Our talk tonight was just foreplay for him."

"In fact, Anson just texted me and said that within the last few minutes, fifteen tickets to the RV showhouse were purchased from the same IP address," Dan said.

"Several of them are for women, the rest for men, and one has a gender-neutral name. We'll check out all of them before race day. Good work."

"Your theory about Adams enjoying the foreplay is probably right," Dan continued. "He was having some fun, hearing your frightened voice and your confession about treating him badly. The department will have all week to screen the purchased tickets, so don't worry. We'll flush him out."

As if he could read her mind, Dan continued. "You're going to be a nervous wreck this weekend, Kim. I've got an idea to help with that. It serves two purposes."

"I'm confused," Kim said. "What purposes?"

"One, to keep you occupied after your shopping trip with Russ. And two, to keep you safe."

"Go on," Kim answered.

"There's a private party Saturday night in the Pagoda Tower at the track. I'm working security since there's so much going on with Adams. The powers-that-be don't want any of the race car team owners to be fallout from Adams's attempts to get to you, and subsequently impact all the race festivities." He took a breath. "My thought is you could come with me as a date, since I'm supposed to blend in. It's hard to believe, but I stick out like a sore thumb if I'm alone, scowling, and surveying the crowd while everyone else parties."

Kim laughed. This guy was funny, even charming when he wanted to be. So, she had a "date" for Saturday night. That was fascinating. She needed more information, though. "What would a woman wear to this shindig?" she asked. "Do I have to shop before this grand event?"

"How would I know what you should wear?" he groused. "Something dressed up, but not for church. Does that help?"

The man was so clueless his griping added to his appeal. "Not church clothes, right. I've got a black sleeveless dress that should work." Kim was also calculating how her bruises would look by Saturday, and how she could disguise the stitches near her scalp. She'd figure it out.

"Sure, whatever. I'll be around for the RV setup on Saturday afternoon, after your picking trip. I can pick you up at home that evening. When we leave, we'll give Tom a show full of hugs and smiles. It'll make him crazy."

"Great," Kim said. "Like he's not crazy enough."

- - - - - - - - - - - - - -

Dan and Anson spent the bulk of the next few days screening the ticket purchases for the RV show house. Due to the high numbers, the tickets were identified with entry times so the RV wouldn't break fire codes with too many people entering at once. Every fifteen minutes there would be another set of gawkers.

If Dan had his way, an RV should serve only its ultimate purpose. To drive a family across the country with minimal fuss. No need for a designer to fancy up the space. "Glamping" made no sense to him. Okay, Kim said race drivers might merit the use of high-end RVs, but that was as far as he was willing to go. "How are you doing?" he asked, as he placed a black coffee in front of Anson. "Do any of our ticket holders stand out as a sick criminal?"

"Several possibilities, but nothing with a neon light on it," Anson grumbled. "I'm about halfway through checking the identities." He pointed to a scribbled list of names to his right. "This bunch doesn't quite meet our standards of safety. And this one," he said, underlining the name, "comes up pretty empty when I plug it into the search program."

"Finley Drake," Dan said. "Unisex name. Few matches on the search." Dan took a long sip of his coffee. "This is him. This is Adams, I know it."

"Maybe," Anson said. "I'm still going to check everyone out, though. There are six or seven others that don't seem like legit names."

"Yeah, do that. But this is him. My gut says it's a sure thing."

Dan paced around the small, cluttered office. Adams was playing and enjoying it way too much. With a name like Finley, they'd be looking for either a male or female. If he showed up. Dan now placed odds at less than even whether Adams would try to get to Kim during the open house. He knew Adams would enjoy the excitement of grabbing Kim while others were present. But it was more likely he would also find pleasure in taking her when she was alone and even more vulnerable, as he had when he'd attacked her in her home. Their plan for Dan to hide in the storage compartment was okay, but not great. Kim needed more protection.

He had a flush of satisfaction that she would be with him at the Pagoda party. Allowing himself a minute to reflect, he could imagine her in a black dress, pretending to be his date and making most of the empty social chat he hated. What he'd give to have that woman by himself for an evening. Not for anything racy, but just to talk and get to know each other. She could be in a T-shirt and bunny slippers for all he cared. He just wanted to be with her.

CHAPTER THIRTEEN

SATURDAY MORNING, AT WHAT seemed like the crack of dawn, Kim met Russ at Cracker Barrel for their traditional pre-junking breakfast. Dan was a few tables away, drinking coffee and picking at a breakfast sandwich. Russ and Kim were dressed for a day of looking through other people's discards. Russ was in his "onesie," as Kim called it, which was actually a house painter's coverall. Kim was clad in her favorite jeans, which were paint-stained and ripped at one knee, not by the designer, but by a nail jutting out from a reclaimed table bought years ago. Her old tank top was covered with a man's shirt from Goodwill. The shirt had been a real find. Lots of pockets, made of wicking material, and sleeves long enough to tie around her waist if she got hot. Sated with their food, they drove in Russ's high top converted van to the antique market in Plainfield. Dan followed but not closely, since he knew where they were headed.

The scent of a typical thrift store greeted them as they entered. A mixture of mothballs, old textiles, stale air, and a whiff of body odor was like designer perfume to Kim. To her the place smelled like bargains, family history, and buried treasure. She had a good feeling about today. Based on his demeanor at breakfast, Russ was anxious to find pieces that would set the RV apart from his other designer homes. He'd said he wanted it to be beautiful but informal, colorful but conservative, and most difficult of all, classic but trendy.

Kim smiled at her friend's impossible vision and said, "What's the plan, Russ? Stick together or separate and meet in an hour? Dan is by the entry, and I saw Anson near the snack area, so I think we're safe if we want to venture out on our own." She paused and added, "Dan knew we wouldn't stick together."

"I think so too, Kim," Russ replied as he looked to the left. "The owner of my favorite booth posted on social media that she's having a sale, so I'm headed there first."

"What should I be looking for, specifically? Any items that you simply must have for your beautiful, colorful, yet classic décor?"

In his typical vague way, Russ said, "You'll know 'em when you see 'em."

Kim loved days like this. She could almost forget about Tom Adams. But not quite. She remained careful while she looked for Russ's required items. She set up her portable wagon and began her search. Her phone was in her shirt pocket, easily reached if she needed to hit the speed dial button that would summon Dan and Anson.

As she checked a Pyrex lidded bowl for chips, Dan sauntered up beside her. "That looks like something from a yard sale," he said. "They want twenty dollars for that? I've seen them go for fifty cents."

After a dramatic sigh, Kim replied, "Dan, Dan, Dan. This is a seventies casserole dish. My mom has one just like it. Her mashed potatoes don't taste right unless they're served from that very dish. It has value, believe me."

Dan smiled. "Your mother must be a great cook, huh? My mom didn't have any special dishes, mostly just paper plates and take-out containers."

Kim relished Dan's eyes as he smiled at her. His face lit up when he allowed himself to grin. "I hate to burst your bubble, but our mothers probably had more in common than you know. My mom's mashed potatoes were of the instant variety, but she put lots of butter and sour cream in them. On occasion, she added garlic powder and a dash of cayenne."

Dan laughed. "But they were good?"

"The best," Kim said. "Whenever we had a family carry-in, the host asked Mom to bring her potatoes." Kim chuckled. "A few Thanksgivings ago, one of the other guests was a woman who had won an award for her bread stuffing at the county fair. Mom was intimidated, but still committed to convenience. So, she microwaved two unpeeled Russet potatoes, mashed them just enough to be tender but with the lumps remaining, and mixed them in with her usual instant but flavorful concoction. Her potatoes were the talk of the dinner."

Dan looked at Kim for several seconds. She wondered what she'd said to earn his scrutiny. Whatever. She was tired of trying to figure him out, which was both fun and exhausting. She had work to do. She waved him off and proceeded to the next booth. He drifted away, pretending to look at an antique work bench located in a stall to her left.

Sixty minutes later, she shared her finds with Russ. He'd come up empty at his friend's booth, disgusted with the meager pickings. "No wonder she's having a sale," he mumbled. "There's nothing but trash left. What did you find?"

Kim proudly displayed her wares. A cast-iron cookbook stand for the RV kitchen won raves from Russ. She'd also scored a red metal cookie jar and a red popcorn popper. Each won Russ's approval, both for their color and retro appeal.

"And look what I found for me!" she said. "A Gucci tote and this toy for Natalie. She loves the Care Bears that Candi and I grew up with. This one's still in the box!"

Uninterested in toys and totes, Russ showed Kim what he'd been able to find. "Asian prints are all the rage. And this will go with the fan I found a few months ago."

Confused, Kim looked at the picture of a Panda munching on a bamboo shoot. "It's cute, Russ, but does it match your esthetic for the RV?" Her question answered itself. The Panda print was going to be awful in the RV.

"As I said, it will go with the Japanese fan I've had for a while. Remember, Kim. Always add an unexpected element to your décor."

Confused, Kim asked, "A floor fan? I didn't know there were Asian floor fans."

"No, silly. A hand fan. You know, for ladies to fan themselves when they risk going from a feminine glow to outright sweat."

"Whatever you say, Russ." Kim knew there was no point in arguing when Russ was in his artiste mode. "I'm going to take another thirty minutes to see what else I can add to the kitchen stuff I've got. See you soon."

Her extra half hour of shopping was worth it. She found several small blue glass bowls that would highlight the popcorn display perfectly. Three storage baskets painted in Russ's favorite primary colors were also bargains. Four white bowls with large red Christmas peppermint patterns were risks, but she knew Russ would integrate them into the kitchen somehow. After all, it was Memorial Day weekend and red, white, and blue trappings were all the rage.

As she turned to pull her wagon back to the entrance where she'd agreed to meet Russ, she felt a sting on her arm. Rotating to see what had happened, she fell on the concrete floor and saw nothing.

- - - - - - - - - - - - - - -

Tom pulled a groggy Kim up and apologized to the shocked woman next to her. "Sorry, my girlfriend has a low blood sugar issue. She'll be right as rain in a moment. Is there a food station where I could get her something?"

After getting directions, Tom instead took Kim to an empty booth tucked several yards away from the main shopping area. He supported her in his lap as he sat on the one folding chair in the back of the booth's tables. Nestled in the shadow of the mall's outer wall, it was the perfect place to hide Kim. She began to rouse, looking confused and suitably frightened when she saw his face.

"Hi, Kim. It's so good to see you in the flesh," he sneered. "Although I'll be seeing more of that delectable flesh when the time is right. I thought we needed to talk a while before our big date. Don't you agree?" He hugged her close and seemed to enjoy the repugnance in her face. Stroking her back in circles, he moved his left hand to the front, caressing her ribs as he settled it near her breast.

Kim, full of wide-eyed fear, mumbled incoherently. "Kim, we need to get to know each other better. Or rather, I need to get to know you. That sorry psych history you did in the ED told you a bit about me, but I don't have any clue about your upbringing or interests." Noting her groggy appearance, he slapped her face, and she became more oriented.

Through her haze, Kim knew she had to get this right. Adams wanted to torment her, and she had to play along. "You don't need to hear about me," Kim said. "My life has nothing to do with yours."

"Wrong. Our lives will forever be intertwined. Your lackluster brand of psychotherapy harmed me forever. As we become closer, you'll pay in a way uniquely suited to you. I'll make sure of it. Your body will respond to my lovemaking while you hate yourself for it. Now tell me, what do you do for fun?"

She took a breath and forced herself not to lash out and scratch at his face. "Fun? Well, you caught me doing one of my favorite things today, Tom. I love going to flea markets. 'Picking' has become very chic these days, but Russ and I have been at it for years. Today we're trying to find last minute items for the RV." Kim took another breath and began to tremble in his arms. "Which I'm sure you know, since you've been spying on me for a while now."

Tom laughed. "You're right, Kim. I know everything you do. It's been fun to watch you pretend you're okay while you're scared out of your mind." He moved closer to her and asked, "What else do you do when you're not being paid for screwing with people's heads?"

Kim was still shaking but tried to cooperate. She knew he loved watching her squirm. Tightening his hold, he stroked the cheek he'd just slapped. More squirming resulted, despite her best efforts to stop. He was having too much fun.

Kim told herself she had to stay strong. Against her will, one tear fell down her face. "I don't mean to hurt people, Tom. I'm sorry that I hurt you. To answer your question, I like to cook and experiment with new recipes."

Tom caressed her arm. "Don't lie to me, Kim. I'll have my way with you on this dirty concrete floor if you do. No one can see us here."

Her mouth opened in horror. Adams touched her lips and said, "But it's too soon. You have to be ready for me to really enjoy the experience. That is, you need to be so afraid you'll do anything I ask. Sound good?"

Kim shook her head, opened her mouth to respond, and he stunned her again. She woke up on the concrete floor, just outside the booth where Adams had held her. Her head was pounding, and she hurt all over. She took deep, cleansing breaths and said yet another prayer. This one was full of lust for revenge, painful revenge on Tom Adams, which she doubted God would answer. She was beyond angry. God would have to understand.

- - - - - - - - - - - - - -

Dan had Kim in his line of vision one moment and in the next instant she was gone. He'd watched her turn toward the corner of the crowded flea market, as if she'd heard someone call out to her. Then she was nowhere to be found. He phoned Anson and had him order the other exit closed.

Several minutes later, there was a commotion a few yards away from his last sighting of Kim. A group of shoppers were huddled around something on the floor. Muscling his way through, he saw Kim lying on the dust covered floor next to her wagon. His heart dropped. He flashed his badge and the crowd cleared.

"I've called 911," an older man said. "I was walking to the booth with the big discounts and almost tripped over her. Is she okay?"

Dan found a pulse and breathed a prayer of thanksgiving. He'd have to analyze that instinct to pray later. It hadn't done him much good lately, but Kim was special. She was worth praying for. As he gently felt her head for injuries, she stirred.

"Where am I?" she asked. "I was ready to leave and then I felt something hurt me. It was like a sting or a pinch." Her face then registered the horror she'd experienced.

"What happened, Kim?" Dan asked.

Kim looked away and assumed the fetal position on the floor. "I don't know," she said. "As I said, I felt a sting."

Dan knew she remembered more but had silenced herself. "I think you were hit with a stun gun," Dan muttered. "Did you hit your head?"

"No, but my bum is going to be really sore tomorrow," Kim said. As she attempted to sit up, she found a piece of paper pinned to her shirt. "What's this?"

Dan looked at the note and muttered again, trying to squelch a profanity. "It says, 'Way too easy.' My guess is it's from our friend Tom." Hating the tears that welled up in Kim's eyes, he continued. "Did you see him, Kim? Did you hear anything?"

"Nothing," Kim said softly. "What does he mean? I'm easy? Easy sexually, or easy to trap, or easy because I'm stupid?" She was crying hard now, but Dan was glad to see the tears were angry, not defeated. He was struck again by the haunted look in her eyes. He was convinced Adams had done more than just stun her. She'd been gone for at least ten minutes, plenty of time for Adams to play his games with her. Bile rose in Dan's throat as he considered the possibilities.

The paramedics arrived with a stretcher and their usual equipment. After checking Kim thoroughly and trying to counter her repeated refusal to be checked at the hospital, they left. "Dan, this is ridiculous. How could Tom have known we were going to be shopping here today? Somehow, he's got my house or phone bugged."

"Or he's tracking you with help from someone, the person who has always been our missing link. Probably that nurse. Plus, it would have been easy to watch us leave with his camera across the street from your home and then have his helper follow us here and then pick him up." Dan questioned his decision to leave Tom's camera at the empty rental but knew if he'd removed it Adams would have found another way to watch and track Kim.

Anson arrived after doing damage control and quieting the crowd. People were back to their shopping., likely assuming Kim had simply fainted. "Dan, I've checked all the exit points. There's nothing that will help us. No shoe prints, no evidence from the note, nada. If it had rained today, we'd be golden. Too bad it's a perfect sunny spring day."

Russ arrived and was nearly hysterical when he saw Kim. "Where have you been, Russ?" Dan asked. He still had his doubts about Kellams's integrity.

"I was in the little boys' room," Russ said. "That rich breakfast food and three cups of coffee, you know?" Everyone winced, even those passing by who happened to hear Russ.

Kim laughed, a little hysterically, Dan noted. "Let's get out of here," he said. "Enough shopping for one day. Russ, you'll have to do the final set up for the RV by yourself. Kim's got a date tonight."

"No, I need to be there," Kim shot back. "Russ and I always get the RV ready together. It will be bad luck if I bail."

Knowing arguing was pointless, Dan shrugged. "I'll be watching from the car outside. Make it quick." Seeing Russ and Kim smile, he knew they'd take their time. The drive to the Speedway grounds was uneventful, for which Dan gave thanks. Again, he was praying for Kim.

At the RV, Russ placed each of Kim's finds in the tiny kitchen, making a cute display of popcorn (which he'd purchased at the antiques fair snack booth) in the colorful bowls next to the popper. The cast iron cookbook stand held court by the cooktop, holding an early Betty Crocker edition. Adele's small cast iron egg pan added to the feel that this was a place for both relaxation and fun.

The Panda print was hung in the living area. Kim almost started to argue about its suitability but knew she would lose. She was too tired to make the effort, and her head was still pounding. Russ then placed the antique Asian fan on the coffee table. The bedroom was checked and rechecked. Towels in the bathrooms were fluffed. High-end shower gel, hair products, and luxurious blow dryers added to the spa-like feel. Russ declared their work finished "for now."

CHAPTER FOURTEEN

WHEN DAN ARRIVED AT her house, Kim repeatedly denied any conversation with Adams. She didn't want to admit what had transpired. She felt dirty, stupid, and violated. The redness from Adams's slap to her cheek had faded enough that Dan hadn't asked many questions. She convinced him that after a long nap, she'd be fine for their "date" that evening. Adele went home but promised to stand watch behind her curtains should anyone but Dan arrive at the door.

She was right about feeling better after a nap. Determined to enjoy her time alone with Dan, Kim readied herself for the Indy 500 party at the Pagoda. Set on the start-finish line of the Indianapolis Motor Speedway, the structure's height topped out at the equivalent of thirteen stories. The building style, with each floor smaller than the one below, likened it to a Japanese pagoda. Those with pricey interests in the Indy500 had access to suites and catered meals during the event. They were also able to host social events like tonight's luxurious gathering.

On a normal day, Kim would have been nervous about fitting in with all the racing elites. After her eventful morning, however, she was only intent on playing her role as Dan's date. She shuddered with anticipation. If only it weren't a role. She could see herself with Dan at various social functions, from events like this one to a simple IMPD departmental Christmas party. She could envision herself with Dan at many other places, most specifically in her bedroom. Blushing, she readied herself for the evening.

Role or not, she hoped her dress would help Dan blend in as a guest. She had paid way too much five years ago for the classic, deep V-neck, sleeveless, well-fitting wool jersey sheath. It had served her well over time. With a subtly printed blazer and scarf around her neck to cover the low neckline, it worked for funerals and professional functions. A pearl choker dressed it up just enough for parties. Leggings dressed down the look, with a bulky belt added for casual emphasis. Glitzy jewelry jazzed it up to cocktail attire. Thinking this affair was at the glitzy level, Kim chose her grandmother's diamond pendant and layered it with a second, shorter gold necklace. Remembering an article she'd read recommending having an odd number of jewelry pieces, she included another thin gold choker. Dangly gold earrings finished the look - dressy, sophisticated, but not overwhelming or trying too hard. She hoped Dan would like it.

While she waited for him, Kim reflected on the work at the RV this afternoon. Despite their shopping adventure, Russ had been more picky than usual, demanding that beds be remade with alternate linens and doing white glove inspections of the kitchen cupboards. Acknowledging his difficult behavior, he'd apologized to everyone as they left. "I'm sorry, guys. Not only are we worried about the success of the RV open house, but a dangerous criminal is out to get us. And I need to recoup my million-dollar investment. What could go wrong?"

Everyone laughed. Adele hugged Russ and said, "Russ, serve yourself a stiff highball tonight. Nothing is going to happen tomorrow. That rat Adams is too cowardly to come at us with other folks around. And I'll have my handy cast iron egg pan on the kitchen counter."

Kim's doorbell rang and Kim's thoughts came back to the present. Dan was right on time. "Hi, there," she said, suddenly feeling shy and uncertain. "Would you like a drink before we go?" she asked as he entered the house.

Dan just stared at her in response. He blinked once, started to speak, then remained silent.

How dumb could she be? He was on the job and couldn't drink. Or maybe her dress was all wrong. Or perhaps he'd had second thoughts about bringing her to mingle with all the wealthy international team owners.

Dan finally found his voice. "You look magnificent," he said gruffly. "I hate that I'm bringing you on a fake date." Staring into her eyes, he said, "We could have a good time if things were different."

Unsure about his meaning, Kim exhaled the breath she'd been holding. She shrugged her shoulders and told herself to get a grip. Either he was interested in her as a person, or he was assuming her jazzed up appearance meant she was ready to jump into a casual relationship. No matter. They had work to do tonight.

"I'm glad you think I look okay. How can I help tonight? Should I watch entrances and exits? Do you want me to walk around and make chit-chat? Should I focus on the men or the women? And which movers and shakers will be in attendance?"

Dan answered with his own shrug. "No, just be my companion, and act like you enjoy being with me. I'll guide us around the party. The movers and shakers are to remain anonymous, but here are some clues. Owners whose last names begin with A and end in I, P and E, R and L." His eyes twinkled. "No one there knows me. I'll only know people by recognition from watching past Indy 500s on television. We'll just pretend we're on the outside looking in."

"Which we are," Kim said. "Are we ready to leave and give Adams a show?"

Dan's twinkling eyes creased with pleasure. "You bet, Kim. Let's do this."

He eased her out of her front door and waited while she set the security alarm and locked up. Pausing under the porch light, he took her in his arms and whispered in her ear. "This is to give Adams a fit." Then he kissed her, deeply. Kim responded, never wanting it to end. Like the kiss in the car when they were stopped on the highway headed to Terre Haute, this one had immense promise. Dan was a great kisser. No one had ever kissed her like this.

Kim finally laughed at Dan's joke and broke free of his embrace. This man sent shivers through her, the likes of which she'd never felt. Sure, she'd had men in her life since Brad, but they were all either bland or full of ego. She'd always been able to keep a part of her soul away from them, separate from their predictability or grand plans. Somehow Dan radiated confidence without being too into himself. They walked to his car, which tonight was not the standard issue IMPD beater but a rented Audi.

"Nice wheels," she said. "Part of the disguise, I guess."

"Correct. Even better, I get to keep it for two weeks, since that's what the rental agency insisted on. They're afraid it will be returned full of bullet holes, so they wanted the maximum rental money up front."

Kim enjoyed the ride from her house in Broad Ripple to Speedway. The warm leather seats and soft jazz Dan had playing lulled her into almost believing tonight's kiss was about them. Just them. But it wasn't. It was about being alert for Adams's presence. And keeping herself, Dan, and all those at the party safe. If Adams didn't follow them and show up, who knew what would await her at home? Better to stay in the moment. That's what she always recommended to her clients. She could pretend a little, couldn't she?

Her phone rang. All thoughts of tonight being fun were emptied from her consciousness as she saw the unknown caller identification. She put the phone on speaker and said, "Hello? Tom, is that you?"

"Sure is, Kim. I wanted to let you and the cop know you'll pay for that tasteless display on your porch. Soon,

Kimmy, I'll be the only one who gets to touch you like that. Don't you remember what we were up to this morning? There's lots more to come, believe me. You'll be mine. All mine." Then the call ended.

Dan glared as she put the phone back in her purse. "I knew he'd touched you when you were gone today." He glanced at Kim's crestfallen face. "He groped you, verbally abused you, and more, right?" Dan pounded the steering wheel and muttered a truly vile curse. "He's predictable, if nothing else. He knows you're somehow 'on the job' tonight and wants to rattle you. How are you doing?"

"I'm great. A psychopath just called me with threats of sexual violence and I'm going to a party where I don't belong. But my date is carrying, so no big deal, right?"

Dan chuckled. "Right. It's going to be fine. My memory of these functions is that the food is very good. Eat something if you can. It will help you relax."

Relax, he said. Sure thing. Nothing to be nervous about. Dear Lord, shelter us with your care. Please prevent me from doing anything to embarrass Dan. Help me be strong and observant. She sighed and realized all she did lately when she prayed was beg God for help. It was time to be thankful for Dan's presence and for all the people who loved her. *Forgive me for my lack of faith and hope, Lord. Thank You for all You've given me.*

After using valet parking, they entered the designated Pagoda suite and found the party in full swing. Kim recognized a few faces from past televised Indy 500 races, noting they radiated power and money. It was also easy to pick out the few drivers present. They were generally small men but still possessed the confidence and bravado necessary for their chosen profession. Remembering the sketches generated by IMPD showing Adams in various disguises (facial hair, wigs, and one even had him made up as a woman), she scanned the room for anyone resembling her foe. Everyone looked normal to her. Adams's height helped her eliminate most of the attendees. Maybe his phone call would be the worst of it for tonight.

Dan took her hand and moved closer. "See anyone you know?" he asked playfully.

"Nope, just some famous folks, the ones you clued me in on. It's very *fancy*, as Adele would say. Another experience for my memory book."

"Let's hope it's a good memory," Dan said. "So far, I'm not seeing anything to worry about."

A loud crash echoed through the room. Party guests looked curiously at the kitchen area. Dan, on the other hand, moved like a cat to the source of the noise. Quick but subtle. Kim stayed put but kept searching the area for Adams.

"False alarm," Dan said as he returned a few minutes later and put his arm around her waist. "Clumsy catering kid. He's hired for tonight only and dropped a tray full of drink glasses."

Kim was spooked. "Are you sure it wasn't Tom? He can change his appearance. He also looks young for his age."

"I'm sure," Dan answered. "This kid was Asian and scared to death he'd be fired on the spot."

Music began to play. The small band's choice of a popular song compelled many of the guests to move to the dance floor. "Let's look like we belong," Dan said. Hand at her waist, he moved her to the groups of dancing couples.

If only this were real, she thought for about the fiftieth time. She allowed herself to sink into Dan's embrace. Moving well together, she nestled her head on his shoulder. She wished Dan were her true partner. They could be good as a couple, him with his fierce protective nature and her with a faith-filled view of life. She knew her faith could be tenuous, but God forgave everything. She was trying, that was clear. Surely God would understand, forgive her, and give her strength to meet her nemesis.

After their dance, Dan led her to the hors d'oeuvres table. Differing from the usual deviled eggs, stuffed mushrooms, crostini, and prosciutto-wrapped shrimp, the offerings included crab-filled phyllo cups, brie with bacon jam, and sweet pea pesto on toasted French bread. She'd have to tell Russ to up his game during the open house, not that there was much time left to change the menu. Kim's food curiosity normally would have relished each and every bite, but tonight she had no appetite. Playing the role, she sampled a few of the morsels. She was sure they were wonderful, but they compared well to wood pulp as they met her dry mouth.

"Are you all right?" Dan asked. "You look funny."

"I'm fine. Just anxious about all we're dealing with. The food is so elegant. I wonder if the Indy 500 organization publishes a cookbook. I'd like to try making some of these when I'm relaxed." She knew she was babbling but couldn't help herself.

"There are probably several cookbooks," Dan said, his eyes scoping the room. "More to the point, do you see anyone now you might be concerned about?"

"No one. The more I think about it, the less likely Adams will come here. He'll know we're looking for him. He's saving his grand entrance for later. And he got his jollies earlier today at the flea market."

"Probably true. Are you sure you don't want to tell me about it?"

Kim shook her head in refusal.

"So, let's enjoy ourselves. Want to dance again?" Dan scooped her up in his arms before she could reply.

She spent most of the next two hours dancing with Dan. He moved well for a man his size, with a good sense of rhythm matching hers. They managed to play the role of a true couple, laughing and clapping for the band as it played the hits of their adolescence. When Dan left to circulate and assess the room, Kim enjoyed mingling with the guests. They were surprisingly friendly, and one woman even complimented her dress. If nothing else, Kim would look back on that memory with a gush of pleasure. She'd made an impression on someone whose net worth was likely one hundred times hers!

Knowing she was being shallow, she asked forgiveness again. God didn't care about earthly treasures. The soul of a man or woman was the crucial thing. Suddenly, she felt compelled to pray for Tom Adams. His soul was infected, damaged, or hungry to be filled with God's grace. She'd never know which, but God did. After the shock of the prayer left her, she was calm. This time her prayer wasn't selfish, but instead sincere. It was all in God's hands. She and Dan would be safe in His care.

Dan was gone for several minutes. Kim looked around at the party guests, wondering which driver would win the race tomorrow. A waiter paused by her and Kim had just chosen a crumb-topped clam on the shell when a man said, "Good evening, miss. How are you enjoying the party?"

Kim eyed the newcomer. He was darkly handsome, elegant, self-assured, and reeked of pricey cologne and money. Adding to his charm, he had an unidentifiable accent that increased his mystique. He stood about six feet tall, so he probably wasn't a driver. She responded, "It's a lovely event. The music, food, ambiance. Everything is wonderful."

"I'm Roberto. With the Girardi team." This sparse information was evidently supposed to be enough to make Kim swoon.

She smiled. "Hello, Roberto. I'm Kim. With the local mental health team. I'm just a guest here, not involved in the racing world at all." Stopping herself, she decided to give Russ some free advertising. "I guess I'm involved a little. I help a local designer, Russ Kellams, with his show-place RV."

Challenged, Roberto ramped up the charm. "How refreshing. It gets tiring to talk of racing all the time. I shall stop by the motor home after the race. I've never met a combination of therapist and designer. What sort of mental health work do you do?"

"Private practice," she said. "Mostly telehealth these days."

Seeing his opening, Roberto moved in for the capture. "Wonderful, Kim! My work sends me all over the world with the team. Do you accept clients with that sort of lifestyle?"

"Of course," she said, surprised that she was becoming bored with the game. "But it depends on their presenting problem. And needless to say, I can't treat those I meet socially."

"Well then, we will need to connect in another fashion," Roberto said, undeterred. "When I'm not with our Formula One team, I make my way to the States for Indy car races several times a year. Perhaps we could meet?"

"That sounds wonderful," Kim said. *Unlikely, but whatever you say.* This man could charm the bark off a tree, sell snow to Eskimos, all those cliches. "Do you have a residence in the US?"

"Yes, a little place on Central Park in New York. My experience is that there are several direct flights between Indianapolis and New York. Or I could have our team's jet pick you up. Your choice."

"What a lovely option," Kim said. Having never known of anyone with access to a private jet save for those on television soaps, she asked, "What's your apartment like, Roberto? I'm always looking for decorating ideas. New York is cutting edge in the design field."

"It's European in feel," Roberto answered. "Reminds me of home."

Kim had hoped for more detail, but she had a part to play, which was to cozy up to the guests at this function. "What do you do for your team when you're in this country, Roberto?"

"This and that," he answered. "There are always problems to solve. I'm what you Americans call a 'fixer.' Would you like to dance?"

She took the hand offered by Roberto and they were halfway into a slow song when Dan appeared from nowhere.

"She can't stay, buddy."

CHAPTER FIFTEEN

ROBERTO GLARED AND KIM started to speak. Cutting her off, Dan said, "It's time for us to go, Kim. Tell your friend farewell."

Kim patted Roberto's arm, Roberto scowled, and Dan grabbed her hand. Roberto sulked off. Annoyed by Dan's possessive pose, Kim said, "I thought I was supposed to blend in. We were just having an innocent conversation while we danced."

"That guy is anything but innocent," Dan said as they made their way to the exit. "He's a major player on the racing circuit. The party is breaking up, and he was intent on taking you home with him."

"You said you didn't know anyone at the party. Who said he's a player?"

"I did. Couldn't you tell? What kind of psychologist are you?"

I'm enough of a psychologist to know when a man is jealous, Kim thought. What nerve Dan had, suggesting her professional expertise was lacking. She was quiet as they left the Pagoda. Dan tried to make small talk and she replied with one-word answers. She knew she was being childish, but she also felt insulted. Was Dan implying she should have predicted Adams's psychopathic patterns? Did he think she'd brought this mess on herself?

As they walked toward the Audi, Dan wrapped his arm around her waist and drew her close. "Players like Roberto latch on to local women like sea gulls dive for fish. They zero in and grab their prey. You're too good for men like him."

Kim was about to reply when Dan's lips found hers. Unlike the kisses in Terre Haute, this one was fierce and a little rough. She responded against her will, and the kiss became more tender.

Dan released her and let her make her way to the passenger side of the car. She thought about commenting on the kiss but remembered his insinuation about her inadequacy as a therapist. No, she wasn't going to say anything else to this difficult man. She'd figure him out later. Her life was complicated enough at this point. The mechanics of trapping Tom Adams deserved all her attention. The drive home was silent.

As he pulled up to her house, Kim said, "You can let me out at the curb, Dan. Tom is probably snuggled up in his bed at the assisted living facility after a hard night at Bingo. He can't man the cameras all the time. No point in putting on a show he won't see."

Dan shrugged and gave her an assessing look. "Whatever you think, Kim. See you tomorrow for the big RV reveal. Be careful when you go to set up with Russ. Adams will try something unexpected. I'll be around the RV before eight, but I may not get to you in time if he pulls something."

Kim got out of the car and leaned into the opening. "It will be fine, Dan. I'll have my phone with its GPS locator if I end up away from the RV. Have a good evening." She shut the door and walked to her porch. She was grateful Dan hadn't insisted on staying to protect her. There was no need. Adams was required to make bed check in the facility. She could be alone and at peace for a few hours.

In a few seconds she was in her home, away from the unsettling feelings Dan had caused. The kisses, those close dances, the chit-chat, and the glamor of the evening had rattled her. *I'm more nervous about Dan than Adams,* she realized. *I've got to get my head in the game before tomorrow.*

She was about to change and get ready for bed when her cell phone rang. Hoping Dan was calling to apologize for insulting her, she didn't look at the caller ID. Or Dan could be just checking on her. Whatever. She'd play it cool. "Hello?"

"Hi there, Dr. Kim," Adams cooed. "Did you and Officer Handsome have a tiff? You were out of his rental car like he was contagious! And here you went and got all dolled up for him. But don't fret. When we're together, I'll appreciate you no matter what you're wearing, or not wearing. Just like our little mini date today. I enjoyed having you on my lap, even though the setting wasn't that romantic."

Kim gasped but recovered quickly. "Tom, you know I was just faking it with the cop. He had to work security and needed me as a cover. You get that, don't you?"

"Oh, I get a lot," Adams said. "See you in the morning for our breakfast meeting. And I've decided we're getting together at five-thirty, not eight. One of my nurses is going to get me out of here early for an emergency fasting blood draw." Adams ended the call before Kim could say another word.

Would this nightmare ever end? Kim burst into tears, got into bed still dressed in her party clothes and jewelry, and buried her head under the down comforter. She prayed again. In addition to asking for safety, she prayed for wisdom. God would help her and Dan. As before, she even forced herself to pray for Adams. That was the hardest part of the evening.

— — — — — — — — — — — — —

Dan drove back to his place without a trace of enjoyment for the new vehicle he'd rented. Kim had gone cold during the drive home. What had he said? Well, his crack about her being a bad psych type probably hadn't gone down well. But she'd been flirting with that Roberto guy with no clue about what a jerk he was. How could she not be aware of that? No wonder she was thick in the mess with Adams.

Whoa. He stopped himself. That was unfair. His cop training and experience told him psychopaths were tough to deal with in part because they were experts at hiding their true agendas. In Kim's defense, she'd known enough to refuse his admission to the hospital when he'd played at being suicidal, or in withdrawal, or whatever else his game had been that night. How could she have predicted Adams would attack her?

He knew guys like Adams. The women who succumbed to their charms were emotionally hurt and between bad-boy lovers, which was probably the case with the nurse at the dialysis center. Since Kim hadn't met those criteria and hadn't fallen for his con, Adams would be ready for revenge. He'd played with her yesterday, stunning her twice and doing who knew what else. All the while, Dan and Anson were impotent to protect Kim. He knew when Adams got Kim alone again the stakes would be much higher, probably life and death.

Forcing himself to be honest, Dan had to admit that the Roberto character at the party wasn't a psychopath. He was a player, sure, but to berate Kim's clinical knowledge because she'd flirted with him was unfair. Dan had asked her to fit in, to support in his efforts to work the party. Roberto had unknowingly helped in that effort. His time with Kim had given Dan the opportunity to thoroughly case the party venue and its guests.

If he were *really* being honest with himself, Kim was a better fit for the party than he'd ever be. She was relaxed, or seemed to be, and could talk to anyone. He'd heard her talk about racing, décor, food, and fashion. Those were just the snippets he'd been able to overhear while he was working the room. He realized she had a level of sophistication that would preclude her from ever being with a man like him. Dan knew he would never be sophisticated; he was just an Indiana guy doing an ugly job the best he knew how.

He had to make it right with Kim. He punched in her number, waited for several rings, and hung up. Okay, she was angry. But it was silly to ignore his call. What was it called? *Passive-aggressive* sounded right. He pulled into the parking slot at his condo and walked up to his entrance. His phone rang. Kim was calling back.

"Dan, did you call me? I was asleep. Anything I should know about?"

She didn't sound like she'd been asleep. She sounded like she was muffled, sniffling, and stopped up. He knew a crying woman when he heard one.

"Nothing's up at this end," he said. "But what's going on with you?"

Kim waited a beat before answering. "Not much."

"Tell me, Kim."

"Adams called after you left. He's still watching me. Or he's got a crystal ball." Kim sucked in a breath. "He knew we were upset with each other." This seemed to remind Kim about what Dan had said. "Well, *I* was upset. You had no right to question my professional ability. Roberto was flirting and I was playing along. Which was just what you asked me to do, actually. There's no winning with you, Dan. I'm getting tired of it."

Whew, she was more than just angry. Red hot, in fact. "I'm sorry, Kim. Very sorry. Everything you've said is true." Time to be the bigger person. "When I saw you and Roberto having a good time, it got to me. Again, I'm sorry."

Silence greeted him. She wasn't going to let him off the hook. "Kim, are you there?"

"I'm here. Thanks for apologizing. It's forgotten."

That wasn't exactly the acknowledgement he was hoping for, but he'd take it for now. In his ideal world, she'd say he got to her, too. No such luck. "What did Adams say, Kim?"

"Just the usual. He knew I was mad at you. He was snide about me dressing up for the party. And he made it clear that he'd always find me attractive no matter what I did or didn't have on. Like this morning." She choked back a sob.

Dan's temperature was escalated to beyond the white-hot range. He wanted to curse Adams and his skill at manipulating Kim. But what she needed now was the voice of reason, not temper. Collecting himself, he said, "Boy, he's good, Kim. He always knows how to get to you." He paused and said, "And he gets to me, too. If he does anything to you, I'll kill him. Believe that Kim. I'll kill him."

"No, you won't," she said softly. "You'll see justice done, which is why I respect you so much. But I'll always be grateful for you defending me from him. Know that, Dan."

The beep in his ear told him Kim had ended the call. What did she mean? It sounded like she was heading him off, as if she were going to deal with Adams on her own. At least she'd calmed down. He'd let her sleep.

- - - - - - - - - - - - -

Kim knew what she had to do. Dan was ready to commit murder on her behalf, which would be against God's commands and would ruin his career in the process. She would deal with Adams in her way, not Dan's. Their meeting tomorrow would happen at five-thirty, not at the open house, and she'd play along, even getting her "sexy on" as she and her college friends used to joke.

She had her own plan, her own weapons ready, and had mentally rehearsed being an acquiescent woman for Adams's benefit. He would enjoy tormenting her, but she was strong enough to play along, no matter what kind of sick foreplay Adams had in store for her. After the attack on her and her friend Russ, her life had spiraled out of control. As a woman who liked a healthy amount of control, she was done with all that. Adams wasn't going to harm anyone else after tomorrow. She was going to take him down and he was going back to prison where he belonged.

- - - - - - - - - - - - -

Adams was awake at four o'clock, thanks to the aide who appeared at his door. "Time for your blood draw, Tom. Seems fishy to me, needing a blood sample off campus on a Sunday," she said. "The driver is already here, so hop to it."

Sending the aide a hostile glare, Adams began to dress. He took his time, knowing there was no blood draw to hurry for. He was tired from the events of yesterday. Almost dressed, he was interrupted by McKinter, of all people.

"Tom, what's this about a fasting blood draw? The aide called me at this ungodly hour because she was curious about your special treatment, as she phrased it. You know we have a lab service that comes to us for these early draws." McKinter scrubbed his face, the exhaustion showing.

"Mr. McKinter, I'm so sorry," Tom fawned. "Angela Hess at the dialysis center thought it would be a good idea if I had my blood drawn at the lab they use, since my kidneys are almost totally healed. She wants to be sure I'm truly well before they send me back to prison." Adams hesitated, then said, "Not sure if that's a good thing or not. I like it here, and I appreciate all you've done for me while I convalesced."

McKinter was still annoyed. "If you only knew, Tom, all I've done for you. Some arrogant detective from IMPD has been all over me. I've had to document all your comings and goings. He even wanted to know when you played Bingo, what crafts you made, everything!"

Shaking his head in faux sympathy for the administrator, Adams smiled. "We have a few minutes, Mr. McKinter. Want to come in for a second?"

"May as well," McKinter said, as he landed on the bed. "I'm up for the day. You haven't had anything to eat or drink today, have you? We don't want invalidate this specimen."

Those were McKinter's last words for a while, maybe for a long while. Adams had the stun gun on full power, not recommended by the manufacturer unless the user was faced with life-threatening circumstances. He shoved McKinter's limp body behind the bed and kicked him hard in the gut for good measure. Assuring himself McKinter's body wasn't visible from the hallway, he checked his image in the bathroom mirror. Adams was satisfied that he looked fine for his breakfast date with Kim.

His "driver" was waiting outside the doors of the Northside west entrance. Nurse Angie planted a quick kiss on Adams's cheek, receiving a more passionate one later when they were out of site of the building. "Thanks, baby," Adams said. "You're a lifesaver, once again. You can let me out at the 16th Street entrance to the track. I'll call you when I'm finished there."

Knowing this was the last ride he'd need from the woman, he winked. She flushed with excitement and pulled away.

CHAPTER SIXTEEN

KIM WAS ALSO AWAKE at four, having slept well once her resolve to end this farce was in place. She dressed in her standard outfit for a designer showhouse, with a few modifications. Her black slacks were a bit tighter than usual, hugging her in places Adams would like. Replacing her usual ballet flats were strappy black sandals with high heels. Her white collared shirt was unbuttoned almost to her front-fastening bra. Instead of pulling her hair back at the base of her neck, she wore it with soft waves and parted on the side. Chandelier earrings, a tiny choker necklace, and bangle bracelets added to her come-hither message. Good thing she was meeting Adams before anyone was at the RV. One look at her and Russ and Adele would know instantly what she had planned. After he got an eyeful, Dan would, too.

With a protein bar and plenty of coffee to give her courage, she drove to the Speedway grounds. Lots of other early birds were vying for entrance, but her vendor pass allowed her easy access. She made her way to the RV, unlocked the door, and after a quick tour, took a moment to admire Russ's beautiful work.

No wonder several race teams were already placing bids to purchase the million-dollar vehicle. Russ told her yesterday he dared to hope the bidding war would net him enough cash to redo his Massachusetts Avenue showroom. Kim had to admit the RV beat the most luxurious hotel suite hands down. Beyond the two sleeping quarters and state-of-the-art bathrooms, the fully outfitted kitchen made cooking healthy comfort meals easy. It was a chef's dream, and it was gorgeous.

Fueled by his need to make back his money from the liquidation of K&K, Russ had created a living space both rich and cozy. After expenses, he'd clear almost half a million dollars if he sold at full asking price, way more if the bidding war was hot. The muted tones of beige and gray somehow worked well together. The buttery soft leather furniture was both masculine and suited to a woman's touch. Even the wall art combined modernistic renderings ("A five-year-old could have painted this," Dan had said about one piece) with soft landscapes. She asked herself yet again how Russ did it. Kim was proud of her home, but it screamed of an Indiana girl devoted to comfort and economy. Russ's décor spoke to the understated elegance of real money.

As she attempted to distract herself from Tom's pending arrival, Kim mentally reviewed her personal purchases from the antique mall. Maybe they would lend a little sophistication to her place. The replica of her mother's mashed potato bowl wouldn't do that, but it was too precious not to buy. Her big score had been two wall art pieces done in muted pastels. Even Russ had praised them as being perfect for her living room. A small victory, but she'd take it. Then Tom had stunned her, and the joy of the shopping experience had been replaced by horror.

She glanced down at the coffee table and saw the only discordant piece in the living room. A woman's hand-held fan with Asian symbols on an ugly gray background was open and centered on the table. Her weak argument with Russ before they left the RV yesterday about the unsuitable object had been fruitless. He'd insisted an award-winning design needed at least one item to keep it off kilter. "Our buyers need to know my decor isn't perfect, and therefore, they can redecorate as they wish. It takes the pressure off them." Then he'd added, "It could come in handy. In fact, a few other things have utility, too." Confused but tired of arguing, Kim had let it go.

A quick check of the RV revealed that things were in place from last night. Adams hadn't entered and spent the night as far as she could tell. It was time for the game to begin.

Lost in her thoughts, Kim barely heard the quiet tapping on the door. Adams had shown up! She touched the flat object in her pocket for reassurance. Time to be a big girl and get this mess over with.

She opened the door and greeted Adams with a tentative smile that hid her disgust. "Hi, Tom. I'm so glad you're here. We can talk in peace." Her stomach heaved as she uttered the words.

He slipped in and closed the door quickly as he flipped the deadbolt lock. "Can we, Kim? Are you sure no one is here to protect you from me?"

Kim noted his tired eyes and bed head hair. *Good, he didn't sleep well either.*

She could do this. "No, everyone thinks we're meeting when you slip into the open house, remember? I'll fake a migraine when they text to ask where I am," she answered. "I'm tired of being coddled, directed, and then berated for doing what I'm told." She looked at Adams, pleading her case with a bigger smile. "It's time we got to know each other as real people, without anyone's interference." She nearly gagged as she spoke, but this was what she had to do. Adams needed to feel safe.

"*Berated?* I'm intrigued," Adams said. Staring hard, he demanded, "Tell me more."

"You can guess most of it," she said, sitting on the sofa and patting the space next to her. She hoped he'd forego a search of the RV for the chance to be close. She didn't want her defense "weapons" found.

Tom complied with her unspoken command, edging close, his eyes assessing her for duplicity. "Tell me, Kim. I want to hear it all. What did that terrible IMPD guy say to you?"

Kim turned to face Tom directly. His face was mere inches from hers. She had to close her eyes to regroup, and hoped she would appear even more interested. "Dan was so bossy about me fitting in at the party. He had to work security undercover, and I was supposed to be his date so he wouldn't stand out. He practically dictated how I should dress and act." Kim squeezed out a few fake tears and wiped them away. "*Then*, when I was talking to a guy from one of the race teams, Dan got all possessive. He said I was acting like a slut, flirting and insulting him with my behavior. There's no winning with that guy. You're not like that, are you Tom?" She nearly screamed at the horror of his nearness but managed to look him in the eye.

He smiled, then inched even closer to Kim's face. "I'm exactly like that, Kim!" Adams erupted. He took her by her shoulders, squeezing them roughly while he shouted. "I'll make the rules and you'll follow them. If you act like a tramp, you'll be punished. You'll dress like I tell you to dress." He surveyed her outfit and jewelry, caressing the thin necklace and smoothing his finger toward her collarbone. "For example, you dressed a little trampy today, but I know it was for my benefit. I'll allow it. And you'll be without those tight slacks soon enough."

"Wait, Tom," Kim pleaded. "You haven't heard everything I have to say."

Adams looked intrigued, arching his brows. "What could you possibly have to say that would change my mind?"

"Nothing. I don't want to change your mind, Tom. Dealing with the detective has made me think more about you. He's such a power-hungry guy." Noticing Adams's continued skepticism, she went on. "And you like your power, too. Right? But your way has finesse and skill. Westbrook is just a bully. He's a caveman, but you're a charmer. I just didn't notice it in the ED. I think we'd be good together. We could go away somewhere. I'm sure you've got it all planned, just without me. How about I tag along?"

Kim gave Adams an enticing smile. She was rewarded when he smiled back.

"Oh, I have plans," Adams said. "Lots of them. Hope you like road trips. We're going on a long one, probably out west where no one sticks their nose into anyone's business. We're going to be a happily married couple, just returning to Los Angeles from our honeymoon."

"Honeymoon?" Kim asked. "You want to marry me?"

Adams laughed as he continued to stroke Kim's neck, moving up to her earlobe. "Of course I don't want to marry you, Kim. What an awful thought. No sense in creating a legal trail."

Scrambling for ideas to extend the conversation while fighting the urge to escape, Kim said, "No, you're not one to get married, Tom. You're much too independent, too open to new experiences. But we can be together for a while, right?"

"For a while. Until I tire of you."

"You won't get tired of me, Tom. We can have fun together exploring the country, doing what couples do on their pretend honeymoons." Kim's nausea threatened to give her away. She swallowed, took a deep breath, and fluttered her eyelashes at Adams.

"Nice try, Kim. You almost had me convinced. However, I know you'd never leave your geriatric neighbor and your best buddy. Nor would you leave your patients. Really, Kim. I'm not a fool."

"You're wrong, Tom. I'd leave my friends in a heartbeat. I'm sick of this city and all its Midwestern judgment. No one would ever understand why I'd be with a man like you. They miss all your important qualities. You're smart and you're a major hunk." Kim managed to blush at her flattery of the loathsome man holding her against her will. Adams inhaled deeply, which Kim thought was a good sign. She forged on. "With regard to my patients, they'd be fine. I have a colleague that would take my referrals. And they did fine without me when I had my concussion. Thanks to you, Tom, I've realized a lot of things."

Adams resumed his grip on her shoulders, but less firmly than before she began her flirtatious speech. Thinking fast, Kim said, "What about breakfast, Tom? You said we'd eat and get to know each other better. I'm starved."

"Good," he said. "I want you weak." He pushed her down to the sofa cushions and was on top of her before she could react, ripping open her blouse.

Adams began his fun by staring at Kim's face, which was full of wide-eyed horror. "Good, you're scared *and* hungry. It's my turn to humiliate *you.*"

"Let's review the night in question," he sneered. "I was a miserable guy with no resources, just asking for a leg up while I got myself together. But no, despite the charm and looks you say I have, Dr. Newton didn't think

I was deserving of her help. You were so condescending! You actually thought I'd be better served by some treatment facility instead of the hospital. That place is no better than a homeless shelter full of drugs, thugs, and bugs."

Kim knew better than to defend herself or even speak. Tom needed to vent. Maybe it would tire him out. She could only hope. His eyes were squinted now, full of hate and contempt.

"Then, when the guy came in full of bullet holes, you all deserted me," he continued. "He was as good as dead, but I was ignored nonetheless." He shook his finger at Kim, adjusting his body as it pressed into hers. "You were a bad therapist, Kim. No wonder your patients didn't miss you when you were recovering from the concussion I gave you. Now you're going to pay. After we're done here, we're going on our little trip, just the two of us, just like you want."

As he pressed in and covered her face with sloppy kisses, Kim fought her queasy stomach and managed to reach around to the small box cutter in her pocket. It opened quickly and with strength she didn't know she possessed, she slashed at Adams's face, missing her intended mark near his eye. She scored a deep cut on his lower right cheek. He roared and grabbed at his wound. She rolled off the sofa and grabbed the pepper spray from her other back pocket giving Adams a face full of the noxious chemical. His anger was fueling his body, though. The pepper spray had little effect. She was too far away from the false fire extinguisher to add to Adams's discomfort.

Still screaming, he managed to get a small gun out of his hoodie. "You'll pay for this, Kimmy." He walked to her and raised the gun, but it wobbled due to the blood on his hands.

As she backed toward the kitchen area, Kim grabbed the first thing her hands found, the ugly fan Russ had added to the living room decor. Closed, the fan was surprisingly firm. She gathered her strength and lunged at Adams, stabbing at his midsection.

Kim hoped she'd knocked the wind out of Adams. But the fan stayed embedded in his gut. Tom hunched over and cursed her. Horrified that she'd actually stabbed another human being, but still afraid Adams would get up again, Kim saw Adele's small cast iron egg pan on the countertop. Grabbing it, she swung hard at Adams's skull, scoring a direct hit to the back of his head. He crumpled to the floor. Kim was about to hit him again when strong arms encircled her. Unable to move, she kicked out and wondered if Tom had brought a helper along to assault her.

"Nice work," Dan said. Letting her go, he quickly bound Adams in wrist and ankle cuffs, while Anson appeared from nowhere and offered her his jacket to cover her exposed bra.

Kim stared at Adams's still body. "Do you think I killed him? I didn't want to kill him," she babbled. "But he was on me, ready to rape me and punish me." She grabbed Dan's arm. "And what are you two doing here? How did you know what I was going to do?"

"I knew you were done with our strategy," Dan said. He glared at her, saying, "Even though it was a good, safe plan, I knew you were going off on your own. So, I spent the night at Adele's house. She suspected you were going to do something rash, too. We saw your lights on hours before you were supposed to meet Russ at the RV. I high-tailed it over here and I had Anson on speed dial."

Adams stirred. Unable to stand due to his cuffs, Dan pulled him up and removed the fan from the shallow wound in his stomach. Kim noticed a metallic point protruding from the fan edge.

"Kimmy, what a bad girl you are," Adams mumbled. "You'll pay for this, you'll see. No one will believe your story. You enticed me to come to this romantic setting." He stared at the cuffs and repeated, "You'll see."

His gaze lifted and he noticed Dan and Anson for the first time. "Ah, the knights in shining armor," he said. "Where were you hiding?"

"None of your business," Anson replied as he led Adams out of the RV to the waiting police car. "See you downtown, Dan. Kim, take care of yourself."

When they were gone, Kim repeated Adams's question. "So, where were you? I did a pretty thorough check of the RV before Adams arrived. I was afraid he would as well."

"Hidden in plain sight," Dan said. "I was in the shower stall, making myself invisible by crouching on the built-in seat behind Russ's fancy curtain. You checked the shower but didn't open the curtain wide enough to see me. Anson was in the storage area under the main bed. Even if Adams had found us, we had grounds to arrest him. He's violated his privileges at the assisted living facility. And he's done with dialysis, so he was on his way back to prison tomorrow. He also used a stun gun on the administrator." Dan smiled. "Not that I'm upset about that fool getting a dose of the real Tom Adams."

Kim fixed her gaze at Dan. "Okay, thanks," she said. "I'm going home to change. I need to be back here for the showing in an hour."

Kim had caught her tormentor, but her face was pinched in anger and sorrow. Why couldn't she be relieved and happy?

- - - - - - - - - - - - - -

Kim changed quickly at home. Always prepared, she had several pairs of black slacks and extra white shirts for showings. She shed her gaudy jewelry and changed shoes, remembering Adams's label of her as a tramp. Knowing better, she thanked God for His grace and for the safety of Dan and Anson. All in all, her plan had been a good one. So why was she so dejected?

She supposed it was partly that she'd gone behind Dan's back. Then he'd done the same and followed her to the RV thinking she'd need his help. What was wrong with them? For a few fleeting seconds this last week, she'd thought there was something building, more than just chemistry, something worth pursuing. She'd been protecting him, after all, so he wouldn't use excessive force on Adams. But in this highest of stakes situation, they were unable to be honest with each other. They shared absolutely no trust. No, she was just a crime victim who required his time and expertise. An ignorant civilian to be rescued. Nothing more.

It was déjà vu all over again when she arrived at the Speedway grounds, though the crowds were thicker. After she parked by the RV, she saw Russ inside. "Hey, buddy, how's it going?" she asked.

Adele appeared behind Russ. "Our question is the same, missy. Dan filled us in, and I just finished cleaning up that monster's blood. Thank goodness he missed the antique rug. We don't open for another half hour, so it's all good."

Kim had to laugh. Then she couldn't quit. Adele's complaint about Tom's blood breached the dam of near hysteria Kim had been holding in. Adele stroked her cheek.

"Your egg pan finished Tom off," Kim said. "Thanks, friend." She took a breath and added, "Let's get this showhouse ready to shine. You need the busines, Russ."

Russ eyed her closely and enveloped her in a hug. "It's okay, Kim. It's all over. You're a gutsy woman and maybe a little nuts, is all I can say. Also, quite foolish, but then what choice did you have?" He kissed her cheek and Adele did the same. "More to the point, where is our handsome detective?"

Kim heaved in some ragged breaths and said, "Don't know, don't care. Adams is under arrest. It's over and that's what's important. They've got plenty of evidence to keep him in prison for a long time." She closed her eyes and willed away the sense memory of Adams on top of her. Smiling, she asked, "And what about that fan, Russ? It helped me take Tom down."

Russ smiled, grabbing his designer suspenders with pride. "It's a self-defense fan, Kim. I thought you knew. The two last fan ribs are actually knives. It did the job, huh?"

"Now I understand. The 'off kilter' design piece was there to help me all along." Kim wiped her eyes again but was soon back to business as she plumped pillows and wiped away invisible specs of dust.

Russ and Adele looked at each other. "Okay, missy," Adele grumbled. "Let's get this man some offers, as you said. But we're going to talk later, count on it."

The open house was full from nine until the start of the race at eleven. They had a few hours to relax and freshen up the place before the second crush arrived after the split-second race finish. Russ was in his glory and ran out of business cards to distribute. Luckily, Kim had a cache of his old cards in the slacks she'd changed into.

She was sipping coffee when a hand touched her shoulder. Jumping, she heard Roberto's silky accented voice say, "Sorry, sweet Kim. I didn't mean to startle you."

"Roberto, what a nice surprise," Kim said. "Shouldn't you be with your team?"

Disgusted, he massaged his temples. "Our engine quit on the second lap. I had to get out of there for a while. I planned on coming to see you anyway. Have you thought any more about meeting me in New York?"

Wondering at the absurdity of the men populating her day, Kim laughed. First a psychopath, then Dan and his macho irritation, then a charmer from Europe. "Roberto, I need a vacation more than you know. New York sounds wonderful. What are your favorite places for a newbie like me?"

Roberto launched into a detailed description of the usual Manhattan tourist sites, then lowered his voice and said, "There will be also time for fine dining and walks in Central Park after dinner. You will love the romance the big city provides, dear Kim. Of course, you must see my apartment as well. The views are phenomenal."

Kim actually enjoyed Roberto's attempt at slow seduction, having endured Adams's cruel assault only a few hours earlier. "That will be such fun! Roberto, we'll have to make a plan when all the race hubbub is over."

"We will," he answered. "Enough about me, Kim. How is it going with the sale of this fine motorcoach? Has your friend Russ had any success?"

"Everything here is going fine," Dan said. For the second time in as many hours, he seemed to appear out of nowhere. "Just a few hours ago, Kim slashed a potential rapist, pepper sprayed him, stabbed him, and finished him off by knocking him out with a deadly weapon." Noting Roberto's shock, he added, "Kim's not to be messed with."

"He exaggerates," Kim cooed. "I just dealt with a customer who wanted early entrance to the RV. It's nothing like he's describing."

"Okay," Dan drawled. "If that's the case, think what she'd do to a guy who wanted to snare her in New York."

Roberto wisely remembered he needed to be back in the pit area with his team for the race debriefing. "Not that there was any race to debrief," he complained. "Kim, I'll give you a call as soon as I return to my home base." Picking up something from the main entrance table, he flashed Russ's old business card. "This number will eventually connect me with you, right?"

"Sure," Kim answered. "Russ knows where to find me." Roberto left, glancing at Dan with a satisfied smirk. *Score one for Roberto,* Kim thought.

She glared at Dan. "You're sure intent on ruining my chances with that guy," she said. "It's really none of your affair, you know. You and I are finished with our business together. I'll give my statement downtown tomorrow. Adams will be up for trial and perhaps then we'll have to confer, but until then we don't have much to say to each other."

"I think we do," Dan said. His eyes locked with hers. "As Roberto said about his team, we need to debrief. You went off plan. You took a crazy risk. You jeopardized the entire case against Adams. You were about to be assaulted and worse." He heaved a giant breath and added, "Yeah, we have lots to say to each other."

Meeting Dan's stare, Kim said, "I'm not the only one who went off plan, Dan. You and Anson were running your own show without me. I got really tired of being treated like a mindless victim with no say in my own life. I guess we're even."

"We're only even because no one got hurt. You were reckless, Kim. How would I have handled it if you were injured, or worse?"

Kim stared. Dan looked different. He seemed hurt himself, almost forlorn because she had taken the situation into her own hands. What was going on with him?

She reached to him and took his hands in hers. "I'm sorry. Thank God no one was harmed, except for Adams, of course. My worst fear was that you would be killed, Dan." Closing her eyes, she whispered, "I couldn't have dealt with that. It would have been too much after all Adams put me through. I had to protect you."

It was Dan's turn to be shaken. "You were protecting *me?* In what universe did that seem like a good idea?"

Okay, he was going to revert back to being the cop in charge. Fine. "My universe, I guess. Sorry it wasn't part of the script you wrote."

"This isn't a game or a crime drama, Kim." Dan released her hands and enveloped her in his arms. "I'm not playing. I've never been this scared for a person I was protecting." Ignoring the remaining customers in the RV, he kissed her forehead, temples, then settled on her mouth. After a tender, lingering kiss, he said, "Please don't call Roberto when he gets hold of Russ. And believe me, he will. I want you to give us a chance."

Kim studied his exhausted face, getting lost in his eyes. "Fine."

CHAPTER SEVENTEEN

FIVE WEEKS LATER, ADELE was puttering in Kim's kitchen as they prepared treats for the Fourth of July picnic hosted by her church. The star-shaped cookies were fashioned from Christmas cookie cutters, with red, white, and blue frosting in place of green and red decorations. Adele looked at Kim as she outlined the shapes with a thin piping tube.

"I've given you over a month, Kim. It's time you quit holding things in and be straight with me."

"What do you mean?" Kim asked. "I'm not holding anything in."

Adele grunted. "Please. Give me a little credit. You're still mad at me for letting Dan stand watch at my place the night you went off plan. As if I had any choice. I knew you were going to try for Adams on your own." The elderly woman's eyes clouded. "How could I let you put yourself in such danger, Kim?"

Hugging her friend, Kim said, "I know, Adele. I took a silly risk, but my logic still holds. And Adams is in jail for quite an extended sentence. If I hadn't met him alone, who knows how long he would have played games with me?" Stepping away from the countertop mess, she said, "If I'm holding back, it's because Dan sweet-talked me after the arrest and has been silent ever since. We didn't even talk after Adams was sentenced. He used me the whole time. I'm just a cog in the wheel of another successful case for him."

Adele then grunted and harrumphed simultaneously. "Gee, maybe he's busy or something. He's got a tough job, and I don't see you reaching out to *him*. You can't be liberated and passive at the same time, missy."

Rather than engage in another debate about women's rights, Kim laughed. "True, Adele. I haven't reached out to him. Maybe I will."

Having reached her limit of nonverbal contemptuous sounds, Adele stood silent.

"All right, I'll call him tonight," Kim said. "I give."

Adele smiled.

- - - - - - - - - - - - - - -

Dan worked at piecing together the evidence in yet another Indianapolis shooting. What was going on in his hometown? The famed Hoosier Hospitality was seldom seen lately. Too much violence, too much death. Not that Indy was that different from other major cities. No, the epidemic of fatalities was more and more common nationwide. What was missing in his country? He had a flash of insight but resisted. The absence of God's presence had nothing to do with it, did it?

He glanced at his missed call log, stopping on Kim's number from last night. She hadn't left a message. Wondering if Kim wanted to tell him she and Roberto were an item, he turned back to his computer. His phone rang, and he was again faced with Kim's name on his caller ID. She was a persistent woman, sometimes to her detriment. He'd have to face her sooner or later. Better to do it now.

"Detective Westbrook," he said.

His dismissive greeting was met with a long pause. Kim finally said, "Dan, it's Kim. You're either playing coy or you've deleted my number from your contacts. I thought it was time we talked." More silence ensued, then she added, "I had to promise Adele I'd call you."

"Well, you can't break a promise to your surrogate grandmother, right? So, you've called. What did you want to talk about?"

Pain filled Kim's voice, despite her obvious effort to hide it with casual banter. "Well, I don't know. Let's see. Tom Adams, his sentence, all our work together to make it happen, our hot kisses during the whole process. We've been through a lot, but you've ghosted me for over a month."

Dan waited. He didn't know what to say. He knew what he *wanted* to say, that he loved her and that she'd been right about God's intervention. Not only in the Adams case, but in his life. But he stayed silent.

"There's no need to review the case," he finally answered, ignoring the most important part of her message. "It's over and will stay that way. Adams didn't only attack you. He was abusive to the younger nurses at the facility. The dialysis nurse even turned on him when she realized how violent he was. When she challenged his increasingly rough behavior in the supply closet, he landed a few punches to her ribs, so nothing would show when they bruised. She kept convincing herself that the stress of going back to prison changed him. Even McKinter had to admit Adams is a psychopath. After he came to, that is. But you know all this, Kim. There's really no reason for you to call me."

The last words were out, and he hated himself for each one. He was a coward. But now that she was safe, there was no reason for Dr. Kimberly Newton to involve herself with an IMPD detective. It was time for the farce to end.

"I guess you're right," Kim said. "I'll let you go."

He heard the beeps indicating she'd ended the call. It was better this way. He was free of Kim's beauty, courage, and intelligence. Freedom never felt so bad.

He was not only a coward but also a fool. After several deep breaths, he made his decision. Punching her number on redial, he called Kim back.

"I'm on my way over," he said. "See you in a few."

He heard applause from the opposite side of the desk. "It's about time," Anson said. "You and that woman are meant to be. Quit moping around and settle things. I can't stand working with you since Adams went down. Too many sullen silences and deep sighs. You're about ready to audition for a part on a bachelor show. Suck it up, Dan. She's worth it."

- - - - - - - - - - - - - -

Dan reached Broad Ripple and parked in front of Kim's bungalow. Trying to delay his talk with Kim, he looked around the cozy street. Broad Ripple Village had come a long way from the party-focused neighborhood of the past. It was destination city neighborhood, home to fine restaurants, boutiques, and music venues. Houses sold fast. Dan mused that it would be a good place to live, still in the city but sheltered a bit from the chaos downtown. Sure, the suburbs held some appeal if a person wanted to be away from the center of the action, but to Dan they were boredom personified. He thought Kim had chosen her home well.

He noted that Adele's house was decorated in patriotic bunting, numerous small American flags, and pots of vibrant red geraniums. Kim's house, on the other hand, was unadorned. It was still appealing enough but there was no display of the summer holiday.

He saw her exit her front door, close it, and stand on the porch with her arms crossed. Her eyes were on fire, and she bent to pick up a fallen broom which she held with the wood end toward him, like a weapon.

"What's so urgent?" she asked. "I thought there was nothing for us to say to each other."

"I was wrong," Dan mumbled.

"What was that?" Adele asked, from her own porch. She had been watering her plants and Dan had missed her.

"He said he was wrong." Kim still looked angry. Very angry.

"Have mercy," Adele crowed. "Based on that little nugget, I'd say you two have plenty to say to each other. Neither of you likes to admit being wrong, you know." She stood up, groaning as she arched her aching back and offered, "I'd be glad to referee. That way I won't have to pump Kim for details later."

Kim glared at Adele, opened her door, and set the broom against the porch wall. She waved Dan in. "I've got coffee made if you're interested."

"Sounds good," he answered. Kim's coffee was always excellent, unlike the sludge at the office. "Thanks for letting me in."

She poured a generous mug of the brew and handed it to Dan. "It took some thought," Kim said. "You look terrible. I decided to be kind." The shadow of a smile lingered on her lips as they made themselves comfortable on the sofa.

Despite her softening, Dan knew he was in for a rough conversation. "Kim, I'm sorry. For a lot of things. We had a terrible time communicating when we should have been open with each other. Most of that blame lies on me."

"Yes, it does," Kim said after a sip of her coffee. "But some lies with me also. I wonder how we're going to get out of such a destructive communication pattern?"

She was talking like a shrink now. Dan realized it was her own defense mechanism. Good grief, he was thinking like a chapter in a self-help book! Back to the business at hand. He moved closer to her.

"I agree that we share the blame in terms of nailing Adams." He looked into Kim's eyes as she scooted further from him. He told himself to keep talking before she kicked him out.

"Part of my unwillingness to fully trust you, or to put you in harm's way, was my sense that Russ was working with Adams. Or that he was arranging the attacks somehow to generate sympathetic publicity for his business."

Kim slammed her mug onto the coffee table. "You're kidding, right? You thought Russ was part of the plan to harm me?"

"He seemed off to me, Kim." Dan tried to capture her hand, but she jerked it away. "I guess I was looking for a twist in the plot, like in a novel or stage play."

Kim stayed silent.

"Look, Russ Kellams was too good to be true for this cynical cop," Dan pleaded. "When a man's ex-wife sings his praises, something doesn't work for me."

"You were looking for a twist," Kim said. Her eyes were finally warming to him. "What you don't realize is that you found the twist after all."

"Not following," Dan said. He took her hand, and she didn't resist.

"The twist is this. There are good people in the world. Lots of them."

He was a goner after that sweet declaration. He leaned in, kissing her gently. "Kim, I think God can help us. What do you think?"

"That's the first time you've talked about God without my bringing Him up first," Kim said. Her eyes narrowed as she studied his lips. "I'm confused. Don't try to manipulate me with faith you don't have."

"I'm confused too, in a way. But I've been talking to the department chaplain and he's helped me figure some things out."

"Like?"

"Like God got us through the situation with Adams while helping me see that I could love a woman like you. Like my faith was always there, but it was buried by all the horror I see on a daily basis. The chaplain helped me see all the good people I come in contact with. Like you, Kim." Dan paused and added, "And he got a big kick out of my twist theory."

Kim's eyes welled but she stayed quiet. She wasn't going to rush into his arms as his fantasies had suggested. He continued, wishing he'd shaved and cleaned up a little. Anson had been ribbing him about his unkempt appearance.

"Like maybe it was God who brought us together, at a time we were both willing to trust another person." He stood and started to pace the tiny living/dining room area. "With my faith getting stronger, the chaplain said I needed to work on trust. Trust in God and in others." He downed his coffee and winced at the burn as it traveled down his esophogus.

Clearing his throat, he said, "Both of our plans to capture Adams were fundamentally flawed. The only reason he's back in jail is God's intervention and protection."

Kim was still quiet. She was the one without trust now. He understood and continued to work on his argument. He also sent up a silent prayer for God to help him convince Kim he loved her without reservation.

"The chaplain gave me some reading, some daily meditations, and mandated that I find a church I'm comfortable with. I've been to three churches over the last month. I've settled on a Christian church downtown, near the library. Do you know it?"

Kim's brows arched and she looked shocked. "I do know it. It's my church. I haven't seen you there though."

"I sit in the back. Actually, I stand to the side in fellowship hall and just listen. And as I said, I've been trying out other places, so I've only been once."

"Okay."

Defeated, he set his coffee cup on a coaster and rose. "That's what I wanted to say, Kim. I've prayed to God that you'd forgive me, and that you would know I'm sincere. Despite our differences, I'm convinced we could be good together. But if it's not God's will, I understand. Take care, Kim."

Kim stood and came close. "I've been praying, too. My prayers have been answered. You're here, you've awakened your faith, and you care about me."

"I don't just care about you, Kim. I love you." He took her in his arms and kissed her deeply, feeling what love actually was. Total. Joyful. Full of promise.

Kim kissed him back. "Me too," she said. "You're infuriating, but that's a good match for me. Adele told me so."

They both laughed then Dan separated himself from the woman he loved and said, "I have one more question. Your answer may determine our future together."

"What?" Kim refused his distance as she draped her arms around his neck.

"Have you been out with Roberto?"

She giggled and kissed him again, with more than a little passion. "No, but I've talked to him. Currently he's speaking to Russ daily, nursing his wounded ego at my refusal to meet for coffee. I finally relented and we've got a date for next week at a restaurant near the track."

"You're going to have to cancel."

"I'll text him back to cancel. But there's good news."

Not caring about any news related to Roberto as long as Kim wasn't dating him, Dan nuzzled her hair and asked, "What good news?"

"Roberto's team bought the RV!" Kim said. "Russ got top dollar after a vigorous bidding war, recouped his investment with a hefty profit, and has six new clients from the open house. God's work again, I'm convinced."

"God's been busy," Dan mumbled. "I'm about to get busy myself."

His enjoyment at kissing Kim's face and neck was interrupted by Adele's sing-song voice.

"Hey, kiddies! Before you get too involved, I've got food ready next door for a lovely meal. We can eat and satisfy my curiosity at the same time." She studied Dan and Kim and added, "Not that I have many questions. Looks like a love fest in here, as it should."

EPILOGUE

- - - - - - - - - - - - - -

FIVE MONTHS LATER

KIM GAZED AT HER wedding ring, loving the simplicity of the narrow band sprinkled with diamonds of varying shapes. It had belonged to Dan's mother and was precious to Kim. Upon seeing it, one of her casual friends had made it clear that Dan was either too cheap or too poor for Kim to consider as a life partner. She had settled that misguided thinking with a firm reminder that flashy diamonds guaranteed nothing in a marriage, as her friend could attest from personal experience. No, Kim thought, there were no real guarantees, except that God was faithful and good. Dan entered the kitchen, still damp from his shower.

"Hi there." He kissed her and sniffed the air. "Smells like a cholesterol party in here. Eggs, bacon, sausage, brie, even croissants. Are you trying to kill me?"

Laughing, Kim nestled in his arms. "No, certainly not. We don't eat like this every day. But today is Thanksgiving, and we won't eat at Adele's until after six this evening. We need sustenance until then."

"Agreed," Dan said. "Did I tell you Anson is bringing his new squeeze?"

"You mentioned it," Kim answered. "He must be serious about her to subject the poor woman to Adele's scrutiny. I hope she's up to it."

"Oh, she is," Dan smirked. "You should be able to guess her identity."

"I have no clue. Is she a sumo wrestler? House painter? Crossword puzzle writer? I give."

Dan smiled. "She's a widow, single mom, and real feisty like you. Funny, huh?"

Kim was lost in thought, then kissed Dan's cheek as she connected the dots. "It's Candi, isn't it? She hasn't breathed a word, except to say she's been dating someone with potential."

"Well, we need to put this new couple on our prayer list," Kim added with a laugh. "Especially Anson, bless his heart."

DEAR FRIENDS,

Thanks for reading *Racing from Danger*. This book highlights the hazards of settling into a cynical, hopeless world view. The problem, for me at least, is that in difficult and heart-rending times that viewpoint comes naturally! God is always good, but more importantly, He enables us to endure more than we ever thought possible. Faith builds strength, strength builds hope, and hope builds confidence for the future and whatever it holds.

Kim and Dan embody this evolution of faith and hope. Neither is willing to give up (okay, they're stubborn!), and they grow in their belief that the future will be better than the present. My hope for you is the same, that life will treat you well, and when it doesn't you will be able to lean on God's protection.

Take good care,
LEANNE

PS – visit my Amazon page for access to my other books: www.amazon.com/author/leannemalloy

ABOUT THE AUTHOR

After a satisfying career as a psychologist and educator, Leanne focused her efforts on writing novels that reflect her firm belief in God's love, grace and provision.

She and her husband live in Indiana. They visit their daughter in South Carolina as often as possible, especially in the winter!

A homebody at heart, Leanne's life is full as long as there are family and friends in frequent contact, opportunities to travel, and books to be written.